"I trust you're on your way to that address you found for Bretton, N3?"

"Yes, sir."

"It's imperative we get Dr. Henry back, unharmed if possible. If not that, then at least before she talks."

"I understand, sir."

"Good hunting!" Hawk said, his breath exploding as he exhaled cigar smoke. "I'm counting on you, N3!"

NICK CARTER IS IT!

"Nick Carter out-Bonds James Bond."

—Buffalo Evening News

"Nick Carter is America's #1 espionage agent."

—Variety

"Nick Carter is razor-sharp suspense."

—King Features

"Nick Carter has attracted an army of addicted readers . . . the books are fast, have plenty of action and just the right degree of sex . . . Nick Carter is the American James Bond, suave, sophisticated, a killer with both the ladies and the enemy."

—The New York Times

FROM THE NICK CARTER KILLMASTER SERIES

THE ALGARVE AFFAIR
ASSIGNMENT: RIO
THE BLUE ICE AFFAIR
THE BUDAPEST RUN
CARIBBEAN COUP
CIRCLE OF SCORPIONS
DAY OF THE MAHDI
THE DEATH DEALER
DEATH HAND PLAY
DEATH ISLAND
THE DEATH STAR AFFAIR
THE DUBROVNIK MASSACRE
THE GOLDEN BULL
THE KREMLIN KILL
THE LAST SAMURAI
THE MACAO MASSACRE
THE MAYAN CONNECTION
NIGHT OF THE WARHEADS
NORWEGIAN TYPHOON
OPERATION SHARKBITE
THE PARISIAN AFFAIR
THE REDOLMO AFFAIR
REICH FOUR
RETREAT FOR DEATH
SAN JUAN INFERNO
THE SATAN TRAP
SIGN OF THE COBRA
SOLAR MENACE
THE STRONTIUM CODE
THE SUICIDE SEAT
TIME CLOCK OF DEATH
TRIPLE CROSS
TURKISH BLOODBATH
WAR FROM THE CLOUDS
THE YUKON TARGET
ZERO-HOUR STRIKE FORCE

NICK CARTER

KILLMASTER

Pursuit of the Eagle

CHARTER BOOKS, NEW YORK

PURSUIT OF THE EAGLE

A Charter Book / published by arrangement with
The Condé Nast Publications, Inc.

PRINTING HISTORY
Charter Original/April 1985

ISBN: 0-441-69180-3

Charter Books are published by The Berkley Publishing Group,
200 Madison Avenue, New York, New York 10016.
PRINTED IN THE UNITED STATES OF AMERICA

Dedicated to the men of the Secret Services of the United States of America

PROLOGUE

Forests, farmland, and heavy security surround the NATO air base in Geilenkirchen, West Germany. Airborne Early Warning and Control System—AWACS—jets roar in and out.

On an autumn evening at this major NATO base, a dozen men and women disguised in tight black pants, sweaters, and caps, their faces blackened against the overhead tarmac lights, dashed soundlessly onto the airfield.

They surprised and killed the necessary security guards, then darted into the airfield's shadows. They checked their watches and waited.

This is the main European base for AWACS planes. From here the converted jetliners cover the four-thousand-mile NATO arc from Norway to Turkey to gather vital information about Soviet-bloc territories. They are crammed with top-secret radar, radios, and computerized equipment.

The base is international, run by the best personnel and equipment from eleven NATO countries. A jet could have a Portuguese pilot, a Greek copilot, an American navigator, radar technicians from Italy, and a radioman from Belgium. Back at the air base in Geilenkirchen, AWACS families eat in a restaurant run by Canadians. Housewives shop in a British grocery store. Men go to the German barber. And anyone suffering from homesickness can visit the American psychologist.

Right on schedule on this autumn night, a big Boeing E-3A Sentry AWACS landed and taxied toward the fueling area. The bustle at the base had quieted. Personnel tired from their day's work and fresh personnel soon to go on duty were eating their evening meals.

After the new AWACS landed, the leader of the intruders nodded at his comrades, and they continued their work.

The seventeen men from the just-landed AWACS crew sat at a long table in the NATO mess. The room was filled with the babble of different languages and the smells of hot roast beef, potatoes, and schnitzel that the Dutch and German chefs had prepared. Hungry, the crew wolfed down their food.

Six of the intruders ran toward the VIP building through the chill autumn air. They passed clean-cut buildings and well-tended lawns and shrubbery. The base was like a college campus.

The intruders slipped into a side door and ran silently down the hall. Overhead fluorescent lights glowed metallically. The leader once again checked his watch, then slowed and gestured to the small group to separate on either side of a heavy wooden door.

The tall, muscular leader pulled the key from inside his black glove and soundlessly unlocked the door. He looked at his comrades, then pushed in the door.

The group burst into the room, AK-47s raised.

The gray-haired woman stared blankly at them, a soupspoon midway between bowl and lips.

On either side of her, the two men in decorated generals' uniforms jumped up from the glass-topped table. Goblets and flatware clinked to the carpeted floor.

The intruders crouched, rifles pointed at the British and American generals.

"Don't move!" the leader hissed in English tinged with a German accent.

He aimed his gun at the middle-aged woman. Her face had gone pasty with fear.

"Out!" he commanded, gesturing at the door with his Colt. It was equipped with a silencer.

She moved a trembling hand to her chest.

"Not on your life, boy!" the British general said.

"You'll have to kill me first!" the American general said. "No punk terrorist's going to kidnap me!" His fingers played with the top of his holster.

The leader of the terrorists laughed.

"Grab her!" he told his men. Casually he waved the Colt at the officers. "No one wants generals anymore. Too many of them. They're not worth a damn!"

He shot the British general between the eyes. Blood spurted into the room, then dripped down the surprised man's face.

One of the terrorists yanked the gray-haired woman toward the door.

"And they're dangerous witnesses!" the terrorist leader went on as the American general whipped out the service revolver from his holster.

Calmly the terrorist leader aimed, shooting the American between the eyes, too. The officers fell against the glass-topped table. It flipped back onto them.

The terrorist leader looked once at the two dead generals caught like specimens under glass. His lips curled, and he followed his comrades and the woman out the door.

The explosion on the airfield lit the night sky into day. NATO officers and men ran for emergency fire gear. The AWACS plane blazed like a fireball, so loaded with explosives that only cinders would be left when it burned itself out.

Shouted orders rang above the fire's roar. Three Italians and two Portuguese raced toward the blaze in fire-resistant foil suits. They carried thick fire hoses. Behind them, more team members appeared to fight the conflagration that might soon engulf other AWACS jets.

"Get that damn plane into the air!" the Belgian captain shouted to the crew in the cafeteria. "It'll never reach Cairo unless you get the hell out of here right now!"

The crew pushed back their chairs and raced for the door. From the cafeteria windows, NATO soldiers watched the enormous flames lick the black sky. Their dinners were growing cold. They'd been watching for some time. They turned briefly as the AWACS crew ran out, then resumed their watch. Their own orders would come soon enough.

As fire engulfed the AWACS jet, controlled pandemonium took over the air base. Pilots and crews sped to their planes. Sirens screamed. Fire trucks and ambulances tore onto the airfield. Heavy streams of water shot into the fireball, making steam but no noticeable improvement as the flames grew hotter and hungrier.

In the disciplined chaos, no one noticed the dark-clothed figures run from the VIP building. They half carried, half dragged a slender woman in nylons, pumps, and dinner skirt. Her head and shoulders were hidden inside a burlap bag that was tied with her arms across her chest.

On the airfield, AWACS and other NATO jets roared one after another to safety in the air.

In the headquarters, the German commanding general was consulting with his Canadian deputy when a soldier burst in.

"Sir!" the young man panted in English, the official language of the international base. "General Hyam and General Butterbaugh have been murdered! And Dr. Henry's gone!"

ONE

Nick Carter moved silently along the dirt trail deep in the Pirin Mountains. It was a gray afternoon, the air cold with thin sunlight. He saw only subtle signs of his quarry: a freshly overturned stone, a few blades of grass springing back, strands of fur caught in the bark of an oak tree.

He rounded a rocky bend and passed a hut and manger made of stones, timbers, whitewashed mud bricks. Ahead on the upward slope, round patches of naked earth smoked. A black-haired Bulgarian man in his fifties stood with two women, one older and one younger, beside one of the burned-off patches. The trio talked in low voices, worried that the unknown vandals who had set the fires while they were working elsewhere would return.

Carter trudged on in his black wool trousers and rubber slippers, just another poor Bulgarian farmer indulging in the national necessity and obsession—walking. None of them gave him a second look, and he was gaining on his quarry.

The explosion behind him shook the mountainside.

Nick Carter, Killmaster, whirled. The whitewashed hut had burst into flames. The man and two women ran toward it.

"Maritsa!" they screamed. "Maritsa!"

The heat and flames held them off, beating them back as they sheltered their faces from the blaze.

Carter dashed past them into the hut. Smoke and fire filled the small structure. He dipped his rag of a handkerchief into a basin of water, wiped his eyes, and held it over his mouth and nose. He felt his way through the hut, searching. At last he found the child asleep in a hand-carved bed, sweating with nightmares and temperatures approaching two hundred degrees. Carter could hardly breathe.

She wept against his shoulder as he carried her out. There was a sudden withdrawal of air as Carter and the child emerged from the burning structure. Behind them, the hut collapsed and the flames shot higher.

"Maritsa!" the older woman sobbed.

"Mama!" the little girl cried and opened her arms.

As the child was swept into her mother's embrace, the Bulgarian farmer pumped Carter's hand.

"How can I thank you?" he said. "You saved my daughter!"

"Maritsa is my little sister," the young woman added, her face still tight with tension. She was in her late twenties, beautiful with thick black hair and skin tanned the color of light honey.

"Glad I could help," Carter replied in Bulgarian. He smiled and stepped away. His quarry would have gained on him again.

"I'd offer you some slivovitz," the farmer said and turned, suddenly aware that his home and plum brandy were gone. "But . . ." He gestured helplessly at the burning rubble. Nothing could be saved. His shoulders sagged.

"Some other time," Carter said kindly.

He clapped the Bulgarian on the back and strode up the trail. He turned once to see the three adults clustered around the child as the hut's remains burned and smoked. The chill afternoon wind whipped the women's skirts and scarfs and the man's big wool jacket. The adults touched the frightened child's face and talked quietly to her in the way of people sensitized by nature. The farmer's family would have to move in with neighbors until their hut could be rebuilt. Their winter would be hard.

Carter picked up his pace. To the right, the mountainside sloped down to valleys of grazing sheep and barren tobacco fields. To the left, boulders, poplars, and oak trees rose toward craggy Pirin peaks.

He pushed on, watching for signs of his quarry as he rounded corners and passed other huts in a series of switchbacks up the mountain.

It was only a brief glimmer, a shining coin of light that caught his eye.

He backed up and looked again to the right on a low boulder. A drop of saliva reflected sunlight like a shiny coin. The dog was tiring and had gone off the trail to rest. Carter moved on after his trained, dangerous quarry.

He climbed around boulders, following a narrow ledge that clung to the side of the mountain. Occasional drops of the dog's saliva led him on. As he crawled over an outcropping of rocks, he saw far below him the still smoking farmer's hut. Below that, tucked at the end of a long, narrow valley hidden by trees and natural walls of rock, was an enormous jet.

Bushes and other shrubbery had been pulled over the plane, but the camouflaging of it and the runway had been interrupted. Parts of the jet were still exposed. Carter studied the jet, looking at the rotodome and markings: NATO-OTAN.

He stared at the great jet in the remote mountain valley and forgot for an instant his quarry.

The dog appeared. A purebred with sleek lines and death in his eyes. He snarled, a deep rumble from his belly.

Carter pulled a hypodermic from his front pocket.

The dog's fangs dripped. He lunged through the air. His lethal teeth were aimed at the agent's throat.

Nick Carter, N3, the premier Killmaster, had faced floods, fires, and fanatics, but never a special AXE-trained dog with chemically enhanced learning abilities. Carter's orders were to take the dog alive. The Bulgarians who'd stolen the remarkable Doberman pinscher had had plenty of time to retrain him into a killer.

Carter ducked, lifting his arm with the thick padding hidden beneath his loose farmer's shirt.

The seventy-five-pound dog hurled himself at the padding and buried his teeth up to the gums.

Carter wrenched his arm free and staggered back. The arm was numb.

The dog flipped onto the saddlebags it wore and scrambled up, growling.

Carter checked the hypodermic and wished he could use a tranquilizer gun on the animal. But the dog had been trained to pull darts out with his teeth or by rolling.

"Remember me, Wizard?" Carter said softly in English. "Wizard . . . Wizard . . ." he called.

The big dog's ears remained flat back, but it cocked its head as if recalling.

"Heel, Wizard!" Carter commanded.

The dog shook itself, and a deep growl again rumbled from its chest. The lips receded to display the shining fangs.

"Heel, Wizard!" Carter tried in Bulgarian.

The dog lunged. The Bulgarians had taught the Doberman to hate his former name. There was still a part in his special intelligence that remembered. But it wasn't enough. Carter would have to take him.

Carter spun away.

Wizard recovered instantly and hurtled into Carter's spin.

Carter fell, his legs twisted beneath him, tripped by Wizard. He lay still.

He heard the dog sniff the air and knew the dog was using his analytical abilities to study the situation.

Carter didn't move.

The Doberman snarled. The dog had decided the downed man was alive and couldn't be trusted.

The dog's nails scratched on granite.

Carter lifted the hypodermic. The dog again sailed through the air toward the man's vulnerable throat.

Sweating, Carter jammed his padded arm between the Doberman's jaws and jabbed the needle into the muscular chest. He pressed the hypodermic's plunger.

The dog shook his head, startled.

Carter's shoulder joint cracked painfully. The animal's jaws clenched and yanked. Then twitched and relaxed.

Carter wrapped his other arm across the dog's powerful shoulders, pulling him down onto his chest. The dog's legs collapsed. The fast-acting tranquilizer would soon sedate the animal into unconsciousness.

The dog whimpered and released the agent's arm.

"Wizard," Carter said, stroking the dog's muzzle.

The Doberman's pointed ears angled to catch the man's voice. Now that he was sedated, the barrier to his memory had been relaxed. The voice was familiar. He licked a wet tongue across Carter's face. He closed his eyes.

Carter smiled and petted the Doberman as he sank into sleep. Wizard was a success. No amount of retraining could eliminate the memory that came from intelligence. It was as strong as instinct.

At last Carter rolled the dog off his chest, got up, and cut the saddlebag belt from the animal's stomach.

Using his sharp stiletto, Carter pounded and ripped the leather so that it looked as if teeth had chewed through. He put the ragged ends between the dog's teeth and compressed the jaws. Teeth marks and dried saliva would make the shredded leather look even more authentic. The Bulgarian agents who would eventually come looking for the dog would find the saddlebags. They'd be grateful to have the useless classified information inside. They wouldn't question that the dog had chewed off the saddlebags and run for freedom. After all, the animal was supposed to be intelligent.

Carter smiled and took a package the size of a small envelope from his back pocket. He opened it into an opaque air-breathing bag developed by AXE scientists. He slid the big dog in, tied the end, and got out the pocket-size radio.

"Alex?" Carter said.

In the distance over the powerful radio Carter could hear Macedonian folk music playing. Alexander Markov was the AXE stringer in Skopje, the capital of the Macedonian republic in Yugoslavia.

"I'm here!" Alex said cheerfully. "Can't come for you until tomorrow. Five A.M. sharp. I won't forget!"

Carter gave him the coordinates and looked at the lowering sun. He ended the call.

Soon the cold autumn day would turn into bitter night. Carter and the dog would need shelter. But first, Carter had to report to the extraordinary David Hawk, head of AXE. He punched the appropriate buttons on the small radio.

"Well, N3," Hawk growled over the radio, "do you

have good news for me?"

"Yes, sir," Carter said. "I've got the experimental Doberman. He remembered his name."

"Damn Bulgarians," Hawk muttered irritably from Washington, D.C. "They're great thieves, murderers, and henchmen. That's why the Soviets love them. But they're lousy creative thinkers. Have to steal other countries' ideas. They couldn't even kill the Pope using that Turkish kid when they had the chance."

Hawk paused, and the radio connection was silent. Gone were the days when static crackled during calls. Using orbiting satellites and AXE's wonder electronics, Carter could call from anywhere on the globe with ease and no interference.

At last he heard what he'd been waiting for—the snap of Hawk's butane lighter. The mighty director of AXE had one weakness—cheap cigars—and he gloried in them.

"Well," Hawk rumbled, puffing happily far away on Dupont Circle, "we'll take a look at Wizard and see whether the Bulgarians figured out anything else but courier work to teach him. Then we'll give him the antidote and drop him back into the Pirins in a week. He'll be just a normal dog again, probably happier. They'll think he ran off and welcome him back. Wizard'll get two square meals a day and a lot of attention. Everyone'll be happy."

"And the Bulgarians will think AXE's investigation into enhanced animal intelligence is a bust," Carter added. "They'll leave our program alone."

"That's about the size of it," Hawk agreed. "I hope that's the last we hear from the Bulgarians. Troublemakers."

"I've something else to report," Carter said.

"What?" Hawk was instantly suspicious. Carter could hear him puffing furiously in his AXE office.

"From where I'm sitting now," Carter said, "I can see a jet that I'd swear was a NATO AWACS surveillance plane. Down in a hidden valley below me. Are there any AWACS jets missing?"

"Not that I know of." Hawk's voice was hard. "But I'll damned well find out. It's curious, because two days ago an AWACS was blown up at Geilenkirchen to cover a kidnapping. NATO is big news everywhere these days. Give me the coordinates and I'll send a plane over, see what we can find out. Maybe it's a facsimile . . . but why would the Bulgarians want one?"

"Yes, why?" Carter murmured to himself before he again read off the coordinates.

"Check," Hawk said. "I'll look into it, but we've got something a hell of a lot more important. I want you to find that scientist—Dr. N. R. Henry. Die Wetterfrösche kidnapped her at Geilenkirchen."

"A biophysicist, as I recall," Carter said.

"Right," Hawk said, pleased with his top man's prodigious memory. "She's been working on top-secret technology dealing with molecular computers and atom-fusing lasers."

"State of the art."

"No one can duplicate her work. It's obvious from the messages from Die Wetterfrösche that they don't know how important she is. We must have her back."

"You want me to rescue her before they find out."

"Imagine the consequences, Nick! With her knowledge—and they'd get it eventually, no matter how tough she is—they could load themselves with weapons virtually impossible to defend."

Carter and Hawk were silent as they contemplated the

power that the violent terrorist group could wield.

"I've only got one lead for you, N3," Hawk said at last. Far away he exhaled smoke. "Not much of one, but you'll make the most of it. A NATO soldier found a charred Hamburg dockworker's quota medal with engraving on the back, 'Stroh, 1963.' Must've dropped from one of the terrorist's pockets when he was stringing explosives along that AWACS jet they exploded."

"I'll start in Hamburg then, sir."

"I thought you might," Hawk said. Carter could hear the smile in his voice, then the warning. "Find that scientist fast!" The connection went dead.

TWO

Nick Carter slung the heavy sack over his shoulder. Wizard, the Doberman pinscher, made no sound. His unconscious body hung like a dead weight.

Carter picked up the dog's saddlebags, then balanced back along the narrow, rocky ledge. When he reached the mountain trail he dropped Wizard's saddlebags on a patch of still green grass a few feet away. The Bulgarians following the missing dog's path would find them.

He turned and retraced his trail down the mountainside. Around him the barren autumn land spread cold and gray. The Bulgarian farmers had harvested their seasonal crops. Now the earth would lie fallow for a winter of self-replenishment. Nearby, in a town nestled on a saddle between two hills, the bells of sheep and goats clanged musically. Mountain shepherds were guiding their animals to mangers. Carter listened, watched, and marched on, feeling in rhythm with the land, the animals, and the growing wind.

He reached the hut that had burned. A woman was poking a stick through the hut's smoldering rubble. It was the older daughter, the beautiful young woman with skin the color of honey. Beyond her was the family's manger, now empty. The farmer had taken his animals with him as Carter had expected. The manger was where Carter planned to spend the night.

"Need some help?" Carter asked the young woman casually in Bulgarian.

He set the sack containing Wizard just inside the structure's opening. She continued to work, then looked up.

"There's nothing left," she said simply. "I'd hoped to find something . . . anything . . . to take to Mother. A remembrance . . ."

She stared at him with intelligent black eyes. She was dressed traditionally, dark braids coiled on top of her head and wrapped in a white *kurpa*, her wool skirt touching the tops of ill-made short boots, her heavy wool jacket bulky over what Carter suspected was a strong, lithe body. She'd had a physically hard life, but the skin on her face denied the usual consequences of an exhausting rural existence. She took care of herself with lotions and makeup. At one time she had belonged to her heritage, but now she looked at Carter with black assessing eyes that knew sophistication.

"You'd better go back before the sun sets," Carter said.

"I go when I like," she said and shrugged. "Where I like."

"Your family will worry."

"They worry anyway," she said. "I'm cold. We'll build a fire. I have shipkaberries for tea."

They gathered twigs and small branches, ranging far over the stony slopes to find enough dead brush for firewood. The trees in that part of the Balkans were sparse and stunted, and timber was in such short supply that much of it had to be imported from Russia.

As she started the fire, Carter slipped into the manger

and injected a weaker, longer-acting tranquilizer into Wizard. The dog must sleep until he was safely with his AXE trainer.

"My name is Vera Georgiev," she said as she set an iron pot full of water on the fire. She gestured at the pot. "Found it next to the well. Funny I didn't think to look there earlier."

"I'm Nikola," Carter said, "from Sofia."

She nodded, not believing him but willing to go along with it for a while. They sat beside the fire.

"Look down there," she said and gestured into the series of valleys that spread below like accordian pleats. "Aren't they beautiful in the twilight? The lavenders, purples. The indigo. From here no one can tell where Bulgaria ends and Greece and Yugoslavia begin."

"Macedonia," Carter said.

"Yes, Macedonia." She rolled shipkaberries between her palms and brushed them into the boiling water. "Once we were the same country—Macedonia." She said the name with pleasure, then looked off across the mountainous panorama. "Why are you here, Nikola?"

"A walk through the countryside. I haven't been in the Pirins since I was a boy."

"You work in a factory in Sofia?"

"Why?"

She stared pointedly at his hands. He turned them, looking at them too.

"You don't have to have calluses to work in a factory," he said.

She nodded. Her face was fine-boned, the nose straight. She had pride, and a confidence few men in her peasant class would ever achieve.

"You don't live here anymore," Carter said, watching as she gathered her skirt to protect her hands from the boiling pot. She pulled the pot from the fire. "Something's brought you back."

"Who do *you* work for?" she countered. "KGB? CIA? Interpol?"

They looked at one another over the fire's flames and laughed.

In all countries at all times, all agents belong to the same family. And until one is sure the other is working on an enemy side, wary friendship is assumed. Only agents depending on wits and information to survive know the constant danger of violence and death, the price of failure, the challenge of winning against lethal odds. It forces kinship.

Carter and Vera shook hands and smiled. Her hand was slender-wristed and smooth from outdoor labor that also made no calluses. Already Carter knew who she was and what she did.

"We'll have to drink out of the same pot," she said lightly. "I have no teacups."

Night settled around them, a night heavy with cold and silence. Only the sharp wind whistling through the scrub trees kept the two company. It was a rising wind, fierce and constant. Birds and insects made no sound.

As the pot cooled, Carter and Vera passed the tea back and forth between them. It was spicy, warming Carter from the belly up.

"You came because of the jet in the valley," he said.

"Word spreads."

"Bulgaria is the most loyal of all the Soviet bloc countries," he observed.

"I don't think the Russians are involved."

"Strictly Bulgarian?"

"Since 1878 we've been grateful," Vera said thoughtfully, staring into the fire. "That's when Mother Russia liberated us from the Turks. Thousands of Russian soldiers died in the fields. Bulgarians think that the Russians' sacrifices are a debt of honor that can never be repaid enough." She looked at Carter. "Whatever we Bulgarians do, it's always with an eye to the Russians. They buy most of our exports. We buy most of our imports from them. The intertwining is endless."

"Where did the jet come from?"

"I don't know," she said. "No one will talk about it. It could be the pet project of a rich member of the Fighters Against Fascism."

"One of the early Communists."

She would continue to investigate the jet. At this point, Carter knew more than she—that it had the markings of an AWACS. If Hawk were interested, he'd send someone to contact her through the Macedonian freedom fighters who lived along the borders of Yugoslavia, Bulgaria, and Greece.

"My husband is a mechanic at the Kremikovtsi steel plant," Vera said and drank.

"Outside Sofia," Carter said.

She shook her head to acknowledge that he knew something of the city he claimed to be from. In Bulgaria a headshake meant yes, and a nod meant no.

"I used to miss him, his laughter and roughness," she said. Shadows from the firelight played across her face. "He always held my hand when I was frightened."

"Yet you left him."

"It was unfortunate," she said. "I was a little girl to him—or a substitute mother. Playing those games degraded me. First I resented him, then I hated him. Eventually I had my own work to do."

"For Macedonia."

"It's what I believe in."

Suddenly her eyes unveiled themselves in the fire's glow. Carter saw the determination to go her own way, then the conflict as her gaze hungered over his face, shoulders, chest, groin, and then back to his face. Passion burned in her eyes. Then—just as suddenly—the passion and hunger disappeared, hidden by her tremendous will.

"What do you believe in?" she said and drank.

"Freedom of choice," he said. "Responsibility and honor."

"Good." She handed him the tea.

Carter took the pot with one hand, her wrist with the other. He set the pot on the ground and pulled her forward. She fell into his arms as if she'd been waiting.

Her lips were hot in the cold night. Her mouth was sweet with shipkaberry tea. Carter ran his hands over the slender body, felt it quiver, sink into him.

He pulled her up.

"I don't want to," she murmured, moving uneasily in his arms.

"No?"

He turned her so that her back was toward the rising wind. Its force cemented her against him, and he braced them both against the gale. The cold stung his face. In the distance, the wind howled down narrow valleys and sang through pines. Nature's elements were rising as if to fight off the night. He felt the power of the earth crackle like static electricity around him.

She shoved her hands against his chest and tried to push away. But her hips rocked into him, rocked as if he were already inside her, and she ravenous for him.

He kissed her again. Swallowed the soft lips. Ran his tongue over the smooth teeth.

"Oh, God," Vera moaned, kneading his chest and making throaty, animal sounds.

She kissed Carter's face and licked the inside of his ear. Her skin tasted of salt and soap.

He flipped up her skirt. She gasped. The cold spread goose bumps over her skin.

He slipped his hand under her cotton panties. She shivered, her mouth slack against his neck. He slid the hand between her legs. He cupped her, picked her up, and carried her into the manger as the night wind crashed and groaned around them.

He placed her on a mound of straw.

"Dammit!" she demanded. "I want you *now*!"

He laughed, hands on hips.

She scrambled up, racing her hands up under his jacket and shirt. Carter stood motionless, thrilling to the hunger in the hands, waiting. Her teeth gleamed white in the faint light of a new moon.

"Nikola!" she rasped, raking her nails across his chest.

Carter grabbed her. Arched her back.

Deep in her throat she growled, a wild sound of desire. Her fingers tore at his pants, clumsy with need.

He'd wait no longer. He wanted her now. This way, her eyes crazed. Her needs out of control.

He flipped back her skirt and lifted her hips high. Quickly she wrapped her legs around his waist. He thrust into her, into the woman of her, panting as she rocked.

Suddenly she shouted. Throbbed. He exploded in a dense heat. Tears streamed down her face. She bit his neck, and he fell with her onto the straw.

Carter tore off his clothes, and they fought into one another, crying out in pleasure again and again as the night disappeared around them.

The next day, Nick Carter stood in a windbreak of stacked man-size crates on Hamburg's docks. He was dressed in a dockworker's coveralls. Early that morning Alex Markov had picked him up on a barren mountaintop while Vera Georgiev slept peacefully in the manger. He'd dropped off Wizard, picked up supplies, and flown to West Germany to begin his next assignment. He'd made a good start. He lit a cigarette and puffed contentedly. The night with Vera lingered with him, and he smiled.

The air above the Elbe River was wet, chill, and smelled of salt and fish. The distant sun gave little warmth. There were forty miles of commercial docks in Hamburg, and Carter had found the one where he hoped his questions would be answered about the kidnapping of Dr. N. R. Henry. It had taken him less than fifteen minutes of discreet questions.

As he smoked one of his custom-made cigarettes with his initials embossed in gold on the filter, Carter watched the orderly unloading of an assortment of crates from an English merchant ship.

Not far from Carter worked Dieter Stroh, perhaps the Stroh whose name had been engraved on the back of the medal found after the kidnapping at Geilenkirchen. The big German was dock boss, bellowing orders and swinging his arms to choreograph cranes, crates, and men as they unloaded cars, produce, chemicals, and clothing in a ballet of room-size cubes and machines. Stroh was in his late fifties, beefy, with a good-natured red face and a broad back. He knew his work, and the men who took his orders liked him.

Carter saw the movement first, saw the crane swing its load too far and too fast.

The other men shouted.

Stroh jumped aside, stared up at the crane operator, and shook his fist.

"Dammit, Werner!" Stroh shouted.

The crate landed hard on the dock.

"Watch it!" Stroh yelled.

But Werner was already back at work, moving the crane's automated cables up the five-story-tall ship. Seagulls circled and called, then dove into the oil-filmed water for greasy lunches.

Stroh returned to his job, too, clipboard pressed against his heavy chest. He stalked up and down the dock, shouting, complaining, cajoling.

Carter ground out his cigarette, then picked up the butt and dropped it into the secret compartment at the bottom of his gold cigarette case. He slid the case inside his coveralls and walked toward Stroh.

"Herr Stroh," Carter said in the respectful voice of the unemployed. He put a slight Greek accent into his German.

Stroh turned at the sound of his name.

The crate whistled through the air behind Stroh.

Men on the dock shouted. Stroh frowned and started to turn to see what the commotion was about. Stroh was too slow and would be crushed in five seconds. Carter had hardly enough time to save himself.

Without stopping to consider, the Killmaster lunged and tackled the dock boss above the knees, skidding him fifteen feet to the side.

The dock rocked as the crate thundered down inches away.

Carter jumped up, quickly followed by Stroh. Stroh rushed toward the crane operator.

"Werner! I'll kill you!"

The crane operator laughed and worked his machine's controls. Again the crane's cables swung up the side of the big ship.

"You're going to need that insurance!" Werner

shouted. "The union'll take *good* care of you once you're dead!"

"You can't scare me into quitting!" Stroh started to climb toward the cab of the crane.

Carter watched Stroh, noting the man's control. This was not the first dock fight Stroh had been in. And from the strength and cunning of his movements, it would not be the last.

"Look at him!" Werner shouted at the dockworkers who were gathering around. "The great union leader won't talk to me for weeks, and now he's trying to *kill* me!"

The murderous crane operator picked up a long steel wrench. He stood in the door of his cab. He glared down at Stroh. Stroh's head was almost level with Werner's feet. Werner held the wrench as if it were an axe ready to chop the head off.

Stroh growled. His broad body went rigid.

Werner lashed the wrench down.

Stroh ducked, sweeping his big hand up. He grabbed Werner's ankle and twisted.

Werner pitched off the crane onto the dock's timbers. He lay there, stunned, his face bleached in the thin noon sunlight.

"You're an ass," Stroh told the man grimly from above.

Stroh climbed down and stood over the downed dissident. Stroh's shoulders squared as he heard the watching dockworkers talk to one another from the sides of their mouths. This was the culmination of a long-standing feud. The union boss's credibility and reputation had been saved, and the men were pleased. Stroh was a man to be trusted. Unsmiling, he looked over the crowd.

"You can't kill the cow if you want to milk it!" he told the men.

As they nodded, the fallen Werner shook his head to clear it. He reached for the wrench.

"Greed will destroy the company," Stroh went on. "Then who'll pay our salaries?"

Casually, Carter walked over and kicked the wrench away. Werner swung a hand for Carter's ankle, but Carter easily sidestepped.

"Go home," Carter advised the man. "You've ruined yourself here."

Werner's lips receded in a snarl, but it was an empty threat. Werner knew he was finished. Carter walked away.

"We own cars, color televisions!" Stroh continued enthusiastically. "Our children go to high school! Some to college! We do honest work. And at night we deserve our beer!"

The men laughed, and Stroh waited patiently, a paternal smile on his face. Quietly, Werner got to his feet and scuttled off.

Stroh watched, then waved a beefy hand at the rest of the men.

"Get back to work," he told them. "You'll enjoy your beer more if you've earned it!"

The men laughed again, and strolled back to their machines and paperwork. Once more the sounds of voices, engines, and squeaky cables filled the cold wet air. The docks handled fifty million tons of cargo a year, and the noise from the work up and down the Elbe River made a thick, prosperous hum. It was an audible symbol of modern West Germany's *Wirtschaftswunder*—economic miracle—that had fueled the nation's ascent to the most powerful financial force in all Europe.

Dieter Stroh took Carter's hand and shook it warmly.

"I'll try to get you a job," Stroh said, his big flushed face sympathetic to Carter's patched but immaculately clean coveralls. "Can't promise anything. Union member?"

"I'd like to be."

"Couldn't have given yourself a better recommendation than what you did today. Werner's a troublemaker. Came to work drunk. I thought he'd got hold of himself." Stroh scratched his short gray hair. "You'd think I'd get over giving people the benefit of the doubt. Had lunch? I'm buying."

Stroh didn't say thank you, he showed it. He was an unlikely terrorist, but Carter had an idea that made him accept the invitation.

The dock boss grinned, then yelled work assignments to keep his men busy while he was gone. He led Carter across docks, train tracks, and paved parking lots. They walked past the city-owned buildings of the Hamburg Port and Warehouse Company where there was an inexpensive canteen. Stroh marched on toward a restaurant called the Heidelberg Inn.

THREE

Pungent smells of sauerbraten, knockwurst, and sauerkraut mixed in the air with the hearty aroma of beers on tap. The Heidelberg Inn was a working-class restaurant where potatoes were heaped on each plate and a mug of beer was assumed for every adult.

Nick Carter and Dieter Stroh sat at a small wooden table in the corner near the door. Men waved and shouted at Stroh, and he yelled greetings back to them.

"Where are you from?" Stroh asked Carter curiously. "You dress like a dockworker, but you're not union." He gestured at the waitress for a menu.

"*Gastarbeiter*," Carter said. "One of the guest workers from Greece."

"Ah, that explains the funny way you talk. What jobs have you done here? Dishwasher, assembler, garbage man?"

"All that," Carter murmured, playing his role for Stroh.

"Now you want to move up," Stroh said, pleased. "It's good for a man to have ambition."

The blond waitress handed them menus. She had bright blue eyes and a filly's slender legs. She smiled directly at

Carter, cocked her head, and walked away, her skirt swaying an invitation.

Stroh laughed heartily. Carter smiled.

"If you attract crates the way you do girls, you'll be the best crane operator we got!" Stroh said and pounded Carter on the back.

They ordered lunches of rouladen, cabbage, and potatoes, and big steins of Holsten beer.

"You been on the docks long?" Carter asked conversationally as their steaming food arrived. The medal the NATO soldier had found after the kidnapping had said *Stroh, 1963*.

"Three generations long," Stroh said, pausing only a moment as pain flickered in his eyes. Quickly he hooded them and dug into his cabbage. "My grandfather and father before me," he said, chewing thoughtfully. "My father was a great man. Helped found the Federation of German Trade Unions. It owns the giant Bank für Gemeinwirtschaft. That's how strong our German unions have got. We threw out the Nazi labor laws and started over. My father helped create a federation of only sixteen unions. No political or religious ties. Now you take England. She's got constant labor trouble and the workers are hungry a lot, but that's because they've got too damned many unions—four hundred and fifty! Ridiculous! Second thing we did was make a reasonable wage policy so money could go back into rebuilding companies. Then, when things got better, we workers got more money. Now we've got work councils, labor courts, and *Mitbestimmung*—union members sit on the supervisory boards of large corporations. See my point? Here 'union' is a way of life. I've got a responsibility to live up to."

"You've got a lot to be proud of," Carter agreed.

"And you like your work. Hamburg is a good city to raise a family?"

Again Carter saw deep sadness rise in Stroh's eyes, and as quickly vanish. It was an old pain that Stroh could control but not forget.

"It's a city of families," Stroh said at last.

"You raised children here, then?"

"The wife and I."

"You have a son to follow you and your heritage?"

Stroh ate the rouladen, cabbage, and potatoes. He tore off a hunk of brown bread, dipped it into the rouladen gravy, and stuffed it into his mouth. He drank deeply from his beer stein. He was a big man who worked hard. He was hungry, and he was delaying his answer.

"Perhaps your son's chosen another line of work?" Carter said gently.

Stroh was indebted to Carter, but still Carter was careful. Stroh was a good man, and perhaps knew information that would help Carter find the American scientist.

"I have a son, yes," Stroh admitted and drank again. "He was a good boy, but then he went to university. Got strange ideas."

"He doesn't work on the docks."

"I'd hoped he would. With his education, he could've gone on to be a union lawyer. Represented us with the right words. He used to love the docks."

"You gave him some of your dockworker's awards."

"He played with them like other boys do tin soldiers," Stroh said, nodding. "Then he changed. Got in with the wrong bunch. Started talking like that goddamned Werner. They're too young, don't remember the unions in Nazi days. Sometimes you have to have it bad to appreciate the good. Life was too soft for him."

"And now?"

Stroh held up his empty stein and shouted.

"Another!"

Stroh looked at Carter's stein. Carter drained it and held it aloft. The blue-eyed waitress picked them off and gave Carter a brilliant smile. She liked a man who enjoyed his beer. It was a traditional German value.

"You must miss him," Carter said.

"I have a daughter, too. Hilda," Stroh said noncommittally.

"Any of you ever hear from him?"

Stroh ate, chewing each bite slowly, slowed by painful memories of loss.

"My father left when I was a baby," Carter said, making up a story. Empathy tended to loosen a non-talker's tongue. "My mother told me he was dead. To her, he probably was. Then he came back one day when I was thirteen. She cried, we all cried. But she wouldn't take him back. She said that if he'd sent word only once—just to let us know he was alive—it would've been different. His silence was unforgivable to her. Worse than if he'd died."

Stroh looked at his plate.

"I know," he said. "She wanted him, but she couldn't trust him. My Hilda heard from Otto three years ago. He told her not to tell us."

"Maybe you could go see him," Carter said. "Patch it up."

"Never!" the dock boss said. "He's made his choice! I won't go to Düsseldorf. He has to come to us!" He resumed eating and smiled slightly. "My daughter is married to a dockworker. I have three grandchildren. Two of them boys." The smile broadened with hope for the future. "They will work the docks! So we skip a generation—the family will go on!"

"Do you wonder what Otto's doing now?"

"Him?" Stroh snorted with disdain. "I wash my hands. Otto could've been a classical musician, that one. He had the talent. Wagner, Bach, Beethoven. Then he played the accordian in beer gardens to work his way through university. I helped all I could. A great musician, or a great lawyer. Whatever he wanted. Now he's probably some bum turning out pamphlets that good people use for toilet paper!"

They finished their lunch and the full steins the pretty waitress brought. It was a good meal, particularly after Carter's meager rations on the trail of Wizard. And then Carter's memories of Vera Georgiev swept over him. Once again he felt her heat, smelled her musk.

"So, like I said," Dieter Stroh said as they walked out into the cool sunlight, "I'll try to get you a job. Go over to the office there." He gestured at a distant building. "Tell them I sent you. They should check with me. Fill out their papers." He clapped Carter's back. "You're strong. Strapping. Otto could've turned out like you!"

As the dock boss walked away, his big shoulders slumped. He'd lost a son to life, not to death. For him, it was a deeper pain.

Nick Carter drove the autobahn southwest through the flat lowlands of Niederrhein. The traffic was moderate, salesmen and wealthy *Hausfrauen* in expensive Mercedeses racing to their destinations through the Netherlands-like countryside. The sky above was clear and the air crisp, but on the horizon hung the telltale brown haze of smog. Germany was paying a price for her hearty economic health.

The sun set orange and red over Düsseldorf as Carter

drove into the thirteenth-century city. Cathedrals, museums, theaters, shopping centers, and businesses were alight and busy in the dusk. The city gave off a sense of prosperous importance and contentment that life had blessed it.

Carter drove slowly through the heavy traffic in his AXE-supplied Porsche. He listened to the impeccably timed motor purr and considered his assignment.

Düsseldorf was less than a hundred miles from Geilenkirchen and the NATO base from which Dr. Henry had been kidnapped. A conveniently close distance. Particularly convenient if the terrorists had a tested safe house in Düsseldorf. They'd need an unusually good one to hide the kidnapped woman from the national and international government investigators who would invade Germany looking for the irreplaceable scientist.

Die Wetterfrösche had been around. The group had formed in the late 1960s and stayed alive despite occasional and well-publicized arrests of some of its leaders. The band had survived intense investigations and supposedly foolproof traps. They were good at recruiting new members, and those who were still free maintained low profiles between politically motivated bombings, murders, and occasional kidnappings.

To maintain a low profile, a person has to disappear—either go away completely, or be interchangeable with any of life's law-abiding citizens. Members of the surviving Wetterfrösche gang wouldn't thoughtlessly break the law. That risk they'd save for their political demonstrations. To lessen discovery, they'd lead lives as ordinary and unnoticeable as any baker, postman, dentist, or housewife.

Carter drove along past the cafés, fashionable jewelry stores, beer halls and gardens, boutiques, and dress and art shops of Königsalle, Düsseldorf's main street. He was looking for a needle in a haystack, but he had sound information from Dieter Stroh about his son.

He parked the Porsche and locked the doors. He inhaled the chill and watched as a group of laughing teen-agers stopped to stare at the forest green car. One ran his hand over the sleek fender.

"You like it more than me?" a girl asked, laughing.

The boy looked at her, his face dazed, and she tugged on his arm. Beer garden music swirled in the air. The group roared their laughter, contagious with the possibilities of the night. They straggled off down the busy Königsallee. The boy looked back twice.

Carter sauntered off from the specially equipped AXE car. Now he was dressed like a well-to-do German businessman in a silk and wool double-breasted suit. He carried three hidden but faithful companions. Pierre, a tiny gas bomb, was strapped to his upper thigh. Hugo, a pencil-thin stiletto, was sheathed in a chamois case on his arm so at the twitch of a muscle it would slide into his hand. And Wilhelmina, his remarkably accurate 9mm Luger, was holstered compactly at the small of his back.

Carter walked with a spring in his step. He didn't know whether he'd succeed in his mission to find Dr. Henry, but the scent of a challenge was enough to give any Killmaster reason to enjoy life. He entered the closest beer hall, the Rhineland, amid the sounds of hearty polka music and stomping feet. The musicians played on a raised platform at the end of the warehouse-size room, tapping their feet and swaying with the amplified music. Beneath them dancers swirled, the women's full skirts radiating circles of color against the men's more somber shirts and pants.

Carter studied the festive room. People came and went to and from the dance floor, bathrooms, and long bar. The musicians ended songs and began new ones. Hefty waitresses carried six enormous mugs at a time, clustered like frothy flowers in their fists. Bartenders behind the bar talked and joked with customers. The customers themselves laughed and told stories at their tables.

Just as the musicians ended a set and left the platform to take a break, Carter found what he was looking for. Two customers—an older couple, probably married—seemed to be sitting alone in the noisy hall, yet people constantly stopped to chat or called to them across the long plank tables.

Every large bar all around the world has at least a couple of regular customers like these two. They are lonely people whose homes are too empty. So they regularly go to a favored restaurant or bar. They seldom make close friends even there. If they could do that, they wouldn't be lonely. Instead, they know many people slightly. Quantity substitutes for quality, and life takes on a veneer of interest.

Carter sat across from them and ordered a Beck's. The waitress was short, round, and blonde, her pink cheeks testament to the kitchen's heat and the glasses of beer she'd drunk. She left with a scowl and a flounce in a display of personality in the crowded room. The couple continued to talk over their shoulders to a small man who had slumped shoulders, watery eyes, and a violin dangling at his side.

When at last the little man left and Carter's full mug arrived, the couple raised their own beers in salute.

"*Prosit*!" they toasted him, then drank.

"*Danke*," Carter replied, and he drank, too.

"You're new here," the woman said and smiled.

She had dyed chestnut hair and coarse features, but she tilted her head with grace, and her hands moved lightly before her as she talked. Her husband watched her attentively.

"You must know everyone here," Carter said with a smile.

"It's good to remember people when you go out, don't you think?" she asked. "So much friendlier."

"My wife likes friends," the man said.

"I'm Eva Dieterich," she said, "and this is my husband Alfred. What's your name?"

"Nikolaus Carr," Carter replied, holding out his gold cigarette case. "Like a smoke?"

"Don't mind if I do," Eva Dieterich said.

They both took cigarettes, and Carter lit them. Alfred looked at his, turned it, and saw the monogram.

"I noticed you talking with one of the musicians," Carter said.

"Nikolaus Carr," the man murmured as he looked from the initials to Carter's face.

"You like music?" the woman said, her eyes alight. "Oh, I do. Very much. That was Kurt we were talking to before. He's a violinist."

"You must be a banker," Alfred Dieterich said suddenly. "A big bank like Deutsche or Commerzbank. You should change your clothes before you come here." He smiled gently, gesturing around the lively hall filled with people in casual and working-class clothes. "You put us to shame."

Eva laid a protective hand on Alfred's arm.

"It doesn't matter what Herr Carr does," she reminded him. "He's our friend now. Perhaps the hall is a refuge for him."

The lift to her voice as she finished made the statement into a question.

"I work for Bayer," Carter explained. "After a day of computerized ledgers, I want to see real people."

"Pills and medicines," Eva said, nodding sympathetically.

"Machines," Alfred agreed.

The couple looked at one another to share their understanding. Without knowing it, they were masterly interrogators. Their genuine interest made people want to answer any question. They would draw out acquaintances, accept and remember any information, then withdraw into their own worlds to savor each tidbit. It nurtured their solitariness.

"I know it may seem strange to you," Carter told them in a low, intimate voice that instantly drew their attention, "but one of my boyhood memories is of our great German classical music played on the accordian. It's a rare commercial musician who can do that. Sometimes when I come to beer halls like this and hear the accordians playing polkas, I yearn once again to hear part of my heritage."

It was the only prompting Eva and Alfred Dieterich needed. They collected information not only to fuel their lonely times, but also so they'd have something to talk about when the opportunity arose. They were essentially without opinions.

"What was his name?" Alfred asked his wife. "Ludwig?"

"Ludwig Bretto," Eva confirmed. "Diabetes. He missed a lot of work because of it."

"He went over to the Bohemian Hall six months ago when he was let go from here."

"Mid-twenties, a nice-looking young man. He was a trial to his wife with his illness. She worried so."

"But he's a good musician—didn't have any trouble finding another spot."

"Used to play some Wagner for us on breaks," Eva remembered.

"He took requests." Alfred smiled into her eyes, then looked at Carter. "You might try the Bohemian. He's a big man. Built like a stevedore. Real good-natured."

Carter smiled at the couple and drank his beer. It was good beer, hearty and aromatic.

"Thanks," he said and shook the couple's hands. "I'll try the Bohemian."

Sweat, perfume, and beer wafted out onto the sidewalk as Carter entered the Bohemian. It was smaller but just as packed as the Rhineland had been.

A group of laughing partygoers jostled past Carter. He felt a sudden furtive rustling in his clothes.

He lashed out a hand. His pockets had just been picked.

He caught the wrist and wrenched it back.

FOUR

Just inside the door, Nick Carter silently bent back the pickpocket's wrist. He stared into a pair of small gray eyes, the pupils dilating with pain.

No one seemed to notice them as the partygoers' laughter merged with the other happy customers at the Bohemian. The newcomers found tables and chairs, and sat beneath a latticework ceiling covered with plastic grape leaves and drooping bunches of shiny plastic fruit.

"I believe this is mine," Carter said.

He took the wallet from suddenly limp fingers. The pickpocket was a slight man in his early forties. Sweat bathed his forehead, but the man was stubborn and wouldn't give in to the pain.

"My apologies, mein Herr!" he said breathlessly. He bowed awkwardly away from Carter's steely grip. "An honest mistake! My cousin . . . we always—how do you say it in German?—we always play the jokes on one another," he explained in French-accented German.

"Is there a problem here?" The maître d' appeared at Carter's side. His face was bored, and his unmoving eyes said he liked it that way. No trouble was allowed in *his* place.

"Nothing we cannot handle," the little man said quickly. The gray eyes darted to Carter and back to the maître d'.

"A slight misunderstanding," Carter decided.

He released the pickpocket and dusted the shoulders of the man's battered suit jacket.

"We'll go outside to discuss it."

"*Mon Dieu*!" the small man murmured softly and massaged his wrist.

He shook his head, held the bruised arm, and stepped back to escape into the teeming room's safety. Carter gripped the Frenchman's arm and pressed him toward the door. "We'll discuss it *now*," Carter said with authority, pushing him outside.

Polka music and the maître d's relieved gaze followed them.

"I'm a poor man in a strange country!" the Frenchman wailed in the cold outdoor air.

"So are we all."

Carter led him around the building's corner into a dimly lit alleyway stinking of stale beer and urine. Broken glass and smashed aluminum cans littered the narrow passageway. A huddled shape wrapped in a ragged blanket squatted cold and low against a wall. In big cities across the world, alleys belong to the poor.

"Hand it over," Carter said.

"*Monsieur*!" The small man drew himself up, stiff with dignity. "You have your wallet. I apologized. It was a joke in poor taste. But you do look like my cousin Jacques.'

"My watch. I believe it's in your hip pocket."

"What?"

"And my tie pin and cuff links. The inside pockets of your jacket."

"I assure you, *monsieur* . . ." the thief said with shocked innocence.

Carter grinned at the intrepid little man.

"Will you get them out, or would you prefer that I do it?" he offered.

The thief blinked slowly and considered. He was dressed in a soft, shapeless brown suit. His dingy white shirt had a round flat artist's collar, and a black string tie dangled loosely from it. The suit was wool, but thin with age. The small man shivered with more than the chilly night. He wiped a hand across his face.

Silently the hand dipped into folds of his brown jacket and brought out the watch, tie pin, and cuff links. All from the pockets Carter had designated. He stared sadly down at the loot in his palm, then offered the jewelry to Carter.

Carter put the watch on his wrist. Pulled down his cuffs and reinserted the gold links. Adjusted his tie and fastened the diamond stickpin in place.

"I usually have more success," the thief said, still stunned.

He had a broad face, short auburn goatee, and intelligent gray eyes set far apart above a broken nose. He tugged at the goatee while the eyes tried to figure out what he should do next.

"You might try a new line of work," Carter suggested.

The thief stood ramrod straight, insulted. The top of his head came to the tip of Carter's nose. He wore hair oil scented with roses.

"*Monsieur*!" he said indignantly. "I come from a family of scofflaws! One does not turn one's back on tradition!"

The impoverished but dapper thief turned on his heel and marched back down the alleyway. He paused at the cold man huddled in rags, threw down some coins that clinked angrily against the pavement, then stalked out into Düsseldorf's music-filled night.

The beggar stared after him, shocked at such generosity from someone who looked as if he might be the next inhabitant of the alley. But the poor man didn't stare long. Quickly he gathered up the coins.

Carter followed the small thief down the alley, stopped to tap the beggar's shoulder and press a bill into his bony hand, then strode on. A shouted call of "*Danke*!" echoed through the alley as Carter left it to head back up the sidewalk in a direction opposite from the thief's. The traffic was sparser but faster and with more horn honking, people eager to get home for dinner or to a bar for a companionable drink.

He walked again into the warm, noisy Bohemian Beer Hall. The maître d' looked at him once and saw that now he was alone. Satisfied that there would be no more trouble to take his attention away from himself, he nodded and turned his back.

Carter made his way to the bar, ordered a Heineken, sat at the end of a long wood-plank table similar to the communal tables at the Rhineland.

He studied the band. There were two accordianists, a guitarist, a pianist, and a bassist. They played a lively polka, and dancers laughed and fast-stepped before them. One of the accordianists was a woman, the other a slight man with a bushy gray beard. He was too old and too small to be the Ludwig Bretton that Eva and Albert Dieterich had described to Carter.

Carter drained his glass mug and held it aloft.

The barmaid who came had muscles that stood out like meatballs on her heavy arms. She wore a black dress, a white apron, and a pencil stuck over her ear, handy to write orders. The pencil was sharp with lack of use. She took Carter's stein and sniffed it, a specialist.

"Heineken," she announced.

"Draft or bottle?" Carter asked, grinning.

"Draft!" she snorted, disdainful that he'd even bothered to ask. "Be right back." She eyed him speculatively, then picked up a stein from another customer and repeated her sniffing ritual without much notice from the customer. He'd seen her do it too many times. She headed to the bar for refills.

Carter took out two bills from his wallet and folded them.

When she returned, she dropped off the other customer's beer first, then came to Carter's table with a mug that was half frothy foam. Even though she'd been surprised that he'd bothered to test anyone as expert as she, she was pleased. He'd given her a chance to show off. She set the beer squarely in front of him.

"Anything else?" she asked.

Carter slipped the bills into her apron pocket. With her, it was wise to announce one's intentions. It was something she understood and respected.

"I'm from Hamburg," he said. "I'm looking for the son of an old friend of mine. He's an accordianist. Ludwig Bretton."

She took the money out, looked at it, then handed it back to Carter. She wasn't ready to be bought yet, but she was interested.

"So?" she said.

"That's all."

Carter put the marks back into his pocket, picked up his beer, and drained the mug. The Heineken was light and full of body. A fine beer. He felt the waitress's impressed gaze upon him.

He handed her the empty mug. She smiled, a woman admiring a real man.

"Ludwig Bretton?" she repeated.

"An accordianist," he said.

She held out her hand. He put the money in it. She stuffed it back into her apron.

"He's sick," she said. "Out a week now. He'll lose his job like he did at the Rhineland if he doesn't find a doctor to cure him." She squeezed Carter's mug between her hands. The muscles on her arms rippled.

"Will he be in tomorrow?"

She shrugged.

"Where does he live?" Carter asked. "I have a message for him."

"Can't give out addresses," she said, then grinned. She pinched the Killmaster's cheek. "Except mine!"

She laughed hard, and her big cheeks and arms jiggled like jello as she carried Carter's mug to the bar. She allowed herself one look back over her shoulder, and Carter saw untroubled loneliness in her gaze. She'd made compromises with life that gave her occasional fun and few regrets. She wasn't going to change now. She turned her square back and resolutely went to work.

Carter left more money on the table, got up, and stretched. Couples necked at tables. Others danced or talked. People came and went in a continuous stream of merry excitement.

He wandered toward the bathrooms. Old and young, the beer hall patrons gave the cheerful room a sense of distilled energy, and Carter felt as if he were skirting an enormous storm of crackling laughter and dancing feet.

He paused with his hand on the bathroom's swinging door and glanced back at the room. He was just another patron, and no one stared questioningly at him.

Safe for the moment, Carter looked up and down the hall that extended on either side of the men's and women's rest rooms. At the end of the hall on the right was a blackboard, time clock, and a door labeled Office. Halfway down the hall on the left was the women's rest room and an exit door that would lead into the parking lot. There was no kitchen, so the staff's activity was centered on the noisy, energy-charged, beer-drinking bar.

Hands in pockets, Carter strolled down the hall to the right.

He stood in front of the blackboard and scanned it casually. Ludwig Bretton's name was listed between Minna Baumann and Hans Bucholtz. Minna and Hans were at work tonight, according to the chalked check marks next to their names, but Ludwig Bretton was absent, an angrily scrawled *krank*! announcing his illness halfway across the board. If Bretton hadn't lost his job yet, he soon would.

Carter noted the lack of staff telephone numbers or addresses, and continued his stroll down the hall, hands still in pants pockets.

When he reached the office door, he pulled out a hand. In the palm was a small ivory case. From the ivory case he slipped out what appeared to be a toothpick.

The footsteps were fast and purposeful, coming into the hall behind Carter.

With amazing speed, Carter crossed the hall in two steps and ducked around a corner. Beyond him was a janitorial closet with a dank, wet mop leaning upside down against the doorjamb.

Carter flattened himself against the wall and listened. He needed information. Trouble might interfere with his getting it.

The footsteps moved at their deliberate, imperious pace down the hall.

Carter stepped into the closet, leaving the door slightly ajar.

The cold smell of the outdoors floated into the passageway. It was a sharply fresh smell, pleasant, preceding the relentless feet.

Inside the closet, Carter slipped out of his suit jacket and stepped into the sweat-stained coveralls that the janitor had left hanging on a hook.

Deception was often a surer path to information than was violence. Carter didn't want to be caught—or noticed.

He zipped up the coveralls, reached a hand and arm into the hall, and slowly and deliberately pulled the mop into the closet. He rattled the mop around inside a rusted metal bucket.

"Is that you, Max?" the voice called. It was a heavy voice, weighted by authority.

"*Nein, mein Herr*!" Carter growled.

He ran a hand through his dark hair and pulled it into an untidy curtain over his face. He hunched his back so that he was inches shorter.

With his foot, Carter shoved the bucket just outside the door. His gait was rolling, almost crippled, as he walked out.

"Max sent me," Carter said, pushing the bucket.

"Stop that noise!" the voice said irritably. "I can't hear you!"

Carter paused, peering up through his curtain of thick hair at a man of medium height with a smooth face and eyebrows so blond that they seemed to disappear against the pale skin.

"Max sent me," Carter repeated, then put the rag mop

between the rollers and rotated the handle to squeeze out the water from the cloth head. "Didn't he tell you?"

"Of course not!" the man said, his eyes narrowing. A smile of vindictiveness hovered at his mouth. "But he'll wish he had!"

"You'd rather no one cleaned the floors?"

Carter reached into the closet for a bottle of ammonia. The other man clenched his fists at his sides. Any janitor was better than none. Carter poured the ammonia into the bucket. The angry man snorted, whirled, and stalked back down the hall.

Carter paused, listening to the disappearing feet ring through the hall. Exuberant laughter and polka music echoed from the beer hall itself.

At last satisfied that he was again alone, Carter stripped off the coveralls and put on his jacket. He walked back to the office and tried the doorknob.

As he'd expected, the door was locked. He glanced again down the hall and saw that it was still empty.

Carter slid the "toothpick" into the door's old-fashioned lock and moved the slender stick around the tumblers. Another of AXE's ingenious inventions, the toothpick's computerized electronics rearranged the tumblers with soft clicks.

Carter withdrew the special lockpick, opened the door, and walked into the dark office. No one would ever know the lock had been tampered with. He closed the door softly behind him.

He slid the toothpick back into its ivory holder, inverted it, and pressed the end. A narrow but extremely bright beam of light shot from the holder.

Carter played the light around the room, noted the roll-top desk against one wall, the swivel chair, coffee table, sofa, and three-drawer file cabinet against the wall opposite the desk.

Quietly Carter walked to the file cabinet.

The office was ordinary, with no marks of distinction to indicate it was the personal possession of any single human. The only specialness about the plastic and wood interior was a series of framed photographs to the left of the file cabinet.

The photos were dated 1930, 1940, 1950, 1960, 1970, and 1980—photos of the staff of the Bohemian Beer Hall, unconscious records of the aging and mobility of the employees through fifty years.

Invariably, the white-aproned waiters, waitresses, and bartenders were stout with good-natured smiles on their faces and mugs of beer held aloft in their hands. Each decade's group stood before the lattice-framed front door of the Bohemian. The faces differed from photo to photo, but the bodies and assumed smiles didn't—monuments to the changelessness of time.

Carter moved the flashlight to the top file drawer, "A–E." It was locked. Again he inserted the small lockpick, heard the soft clicks, then opened the drawer.

Ludwig Bretton's file was near the front.

Carter memorized Bretton's apartment address, then read the rest of the file. Bretton was twenty-eight, married to Lina Baer, no children. Had played the accordian at the Rhineland for three years, and before that in several beer halls in Munich. He listed his interests as reading and attending dramas such as those at the Schauspielhaus. He said he had only a high school education. Under "Aspirations," he'd written "World peace, no matter what the cost." The blanks were filled with writing in the cramped, nearly unreadable scribbles of the mean-spirited and opinionated. Ludwig Bretton promised to be a tenacious adversary.

Carter closed the file, reinserted it in its alphabetical place, and shut the drawer. He ran the toothpick over the tumblers, locking the file drawer again.

As he walked back across the office, he moved the flashlight's strong beam over the furniture, checking once more that he'd disturbed nothing.

It was the sound of the door's hinges and the crack of light from the hallway that alerted him.

The door had opened swiftly, and just as swiftly Carter had Wilhelmina in his hand.

He dived behind the desk.

The explosion in the office was small, as if contained under glass.

Carter leaped up. He didn't have a gas mask. He took a deep breath and raced through orange and gray smoke toward the door, wondering whether it had been the hefty barmaid or the disgruntled boss who'd told the wrong person about his presence.

Almost instantly he felt the fumes on his skin. He was in trouble. It was the kind of gas that didn't have to be inhaled.

He crashed through the door, Wilhelmina raised.

Rough hands grabbed him.

He struggled to turn, fight, shoot, escape.

Too late. His skin had absorbed the gas. He collapsed in the hands waiting for him.

FIVE

On his right side, Nick Carter burned with the intensity of an oven, his body too hot to touch.

On his left side, Carter froze. The skin rose in mounds of goose bumps. That side was growing numb.

In his dreams, Carter was outwitting a monster. He smelled its fetid breath and heard its joints grind as it stalked him. Each time that Carter escaped, his head throbbed with the effort.

"Some Killmaster!" a man said in German.

There was viciousness in the voice, followed by the deep guffawing laughter of several men.

In the dream, Carter whirled and charged the gargantuan monster. Its lethal green claws sliced the air. Carter dodged, came in under the razor-sharp attack, and pushed Wilhelmina up into the soft pasty underbelly. Instantly the wily monster collapsed onto Carter.

"Capitalism once again proves that King Profit builds stupid men!"

The didactic voice was a fundamentalist preacher's, or an unreasoning fanatic's. The men who listened roared their appreciation. Their laughter vibrated and echoed in such a way that Carter even in the haze of his unconscious knew the room was small.

In the dream, Carter was suffocating under the monster's gummy flesh. Carter's lungs burned with the need for oxygen. He had to move quickly or he'd die. He pushed Wilhelmina to arm's length somewhere in the monster's vast belly. He guessed where the heart was, aimed, and squeezed the trigger.

"Of course, communism's no better!" the voice went on pompously. "Blind idiots following a State that hasn't yet heard of individual justice. Bureaucrat is synonymous with baboon!"

The monster's flesh exploded, a hot boil bursting. Vile green and black wastes drenched Carter, filling his nose and ears. He shook like a dog and coughed away the monster's clotting filth. His head was swollen with pain.

"He's awake!" another voice said.

Carter fought up from the diseased monster's stinking remains, away from the plague of the worst disease—fear.

"Good," the first voice said, as satisfied as if he'd brought Carter back to consciousness himself. "Now the pig will talk!"

Carter opened his eyes, moving them slowly, respecting his throbbing head. His hands were bound behind him with ropes that pinned him flat and upright against the rough wood of what had probably been a tabletop. The tabletop was leaning against a wall in a basement that had been shelled long ago, probably during the war. In both West and East Germany, *the* war was World War II. Stones from the basement's walls had tumbled in, spread and stacked as if by a careless child. The hole stank of garbage and human waste, a shelter for forty years for vagrants and the dispossessed. Above, through broken timbers and the first floor's ripped-up planks, the stars shone cold and distant.

"Headache bad?" the man who owned the first voice inquired cruelly.

On Carter's right side an open fire burned, roasting him there, while the rest of him froze in the frigid German night. Another man, still unconscious, was also tied to planks. He was propped against the wall on the other side of the fire. His face was battered, black dried blood on his cheeks and temples from beatings.

"A gas headache is bad," the man with the first voice went on, pleased that Carter was in pain. His smile was broad and knowing, and he held Wilhelmina dangling conveniently at his side.

"It's suddenly gotten better," Carter said and smiled back into steely blue eyes. The smile sent shudders of pain through his nervous system, but he refused to even flinch. "Friends of Ludwig Bretton?"

The man's smile evaporated. He was very thin, trembling with intensity. He wore rimless glasses and had the stooped stance of a man who read too much and thought too little. He wanted to ask Carter how he knew they were after him because of Bretton, but asking would've shown weakness.

"An easy deduction," Carter said helpfully, reading the man's mind. "If it wasn't the barmaid, it was the suspicious manager. Some of you probably work there too."

There were three men with the leader, all dressed in worn jackets and jeans, tattered and greasy. The men's scruffiness was a statement of disillusionment and disregard for societal expectations. They lounged arrogantly against walls, submachine guns across their arms, as they stared at their bound quarry with the satisfaction of men whose dinner has been served on a sterling platter.

"Glad you found me," Carter said, smiling at the hopelessness of the gesture in the men's studied poses and clothes.

The three men looked at their leader. They were surprised by the aplomb of a man at their mercy.

"You won't be glad for long!" the bone-thin leader said and pressed Wilhelmina's barrel into Carter's neck. "What do you want Bretton for?"

"The hunt was too easy," Carter said casually.

Expertly he pulled against the ropes without the men's noticing. The bindings were tight, unmovable, and the knots were hidden out of reach behind the tabletop. Without weapons or help, escape would be impossible.

"Boring," Carter finished.

The leader stared at Carter a moment, then pulled Wilhelmina away from Carter's neck. He gazed at the gun from barrel to handle, hefted it, balanced it, caressed it with the fingers of his other hand. Once again he looked at Carter, an evil smile playing at the corners of his mouth.

"Rheinhold wanted me to kill you," he said.

Suddenly the leader's hand lashed out, quick as a cobra, and struck Carter's face so his skull smashed against the rough tabletop. Carter's ears rang. His head exploded with red-hot pain.

"Didn't you, Rheinhold?"

The man named Rheinhold laughed, his lips thin and flat against rotted teeth.

"I'll do it, Konrad! Let me!"

"But I told Rheinhold that you could buy your life with answers. Didn't I tell you that, Rheinhold?"

Rheinhold nodded, disappointed until an idea struck him.

"He won't talk," he decided. "You can have the other one."

His gaze flickered in the direction of the unconscious man. The man was moaning softly.

"It's my turn!" Rheinhold continued.

"Is it really?"

"Yes, yes!"

"Sorry. Must've lost count."

Konrad returned his attention to Carter.

"You can see how it is," he told him. "I have to keep my men happy."

"A wise leader," Carter agreed sarcastically.

The hand lashed out again, striking Carter's face once, twice, and a third time. The pain reverberated through Carter like an electric shock.

"*Wasser* . . ." moaned the other bound man. He licked his dry lips and shuddered. "*Wasser, bitte*!"

The leader, Konrad, motioned to Rheinhold, and the two of them drew close to the man who was regaining consciousness. The man was plump and soft, wearing a black business suit and white tie. The ropes taut across his thick body caught his trousers so that his thick black socks showed above heavy-soled shoes.

"No money, no water!" Konrad shouted at the man. "Some errand boy!"

The fat man's eyes opened, little beady bird eyes that shifted around the basement hole.

"I thought it was in the suitcase," the fat man groaned. His German was accented. "They told me it was in the suitcase!"

Konrad kicked a cheap cardboard suitcase into the fire. Ashes gusted into the air, and flames soared as they caught the dry case and burned vigorously.

Konrad watched, then leaned toward the fat man, his

nose inches away. Shadows from the fire played across the two men's faces—one terrified, the other furious.

"You, you bastard," Konrad said coldly. "You stole it!"

"No! No one would be so stupid!"

"Where did you hide it?"

"I didn't! I didn't!"

Rheinhold grinned, then slammed a fist the size of a ham into the man's stomach.

The man pitched against the ropes, his face blue.

"Where is it?" Konrad demanded. He slapped the fat man's cheeks, the blows fast and slicing as a whip's.

Tears of pain and humiliation streamed down the foreigner's cheeks. He gasped for air.

"They . . . tricked . . . me . . ."

Now Carter recognized the accent. It was Bulgarian.

"Bah!" Konrad exploded. He stalked away.

Rheinhold looked after his leader, then grinned at the two other men. They closed in on the fat man.

"No!" the fat man cried, trying to fade back into the boards behind him.

Carter moved his wrist, feeling for Hugo. Had his captors found it?

Rheinhold made fists of his enormous hands and pounded the fat man's rib cage. The man writhed and cried out. Rheinhold dusted his hands, proud of his idea of professionalism, and stepped back.

Quickly the other two men stepped forward. The first blasted two fast blows up into the fat man's spleen. Again he cried out. The second kneed him in the groin, then shot an upper cut into the jaw that sent his head into a sharp crack against the planks. The head fell forward limply.

"Wait!" Konrad called out.

The stiletto was still strapped to Carter's forearm. But

the ropes were too tight for him to flip it into his hand. Slowly he worked the arm back and forth, millimeters of an inch at a time.

His chin jutting out and his eyes narrowed, the leader stalked toward the collapsed man. He grabbed a handful of the fat man's hair and yanked up the head.

"Look at me, dammit!" Konrad snarled, waiting for the fat man's eyes to focus. "If you *didn't* steal it, then your friends had no intention of paying us at all! Why are they bothering to negotiate?"

"I . . . don't . . . know . . ."

The fat man's voice faded and his eyes closed.

"Shit!" The leader released the hair, and the man's head fell, chin on his chest.

Carter's ropes were loosening. Not much, but with work he had a chance.

Konrad glared at the unconscious man a moment longer as if by the power of his own will he could force the man to come to and talk. At last he spat on the ground and turned burning eyes on Carter.

"You won't escape so easily!" he vowed.

The three German toughs joined their leader and circled around Nick Carter like hungry strays around a bone. They knew they were going to share, but they wouldn't let that ruin their pleasure.

"The brave Wetterfrösche, I presume?" Carter said.

"If Killmasters are so smart, how come they're caught so easily?" Konrad sneered. His men laughed eagerly.

"I assume you chose your name because you want to be like the Weathermen gang in the United States," Carter went on. He wanted to keep them talking long enough to secretly work loose the ropes around his wrist. "The Weathermen are impotent now. Dead. In jail. The other survivors reformed and are trying to find jobs, raise their families. I doubt you'll be so lucky."

"They were the starting point," Konrad said. "They showed us it could be done. We learned by their example—and their mistakes. Power is abused by corrupt governments. The only way to destroy that corruption is to fight it like it fights the truth!"

"And what will you end up with? More corrupt power abusing the citizens you want to rule."

The three men were watching their leader curiously but impatiently. Die Wetterfrösche to them was only an excuse for violence.

"Ever hear of Gandhi?" Carter asked. "Of civil disobedience? You might get arrested, but your message would be taken seriously. How do you expect the world to believe your sincerity when it's punctuated by the deaths of innocent people?"

Konrad's face went ash white in the glare of the open fire. Debating wasn't his long suit. And what he couldn't do made him angry with frustration.

"It's no good arguing with a paid killer!" he said, shaking with rage. "That's where your title comes from—*Kill*master!" he shouted.

"I work for my government," Carter said. His wrist was raw, but the ropes were still loosening. "The same government that rebuilt West Germany into one of the most comfortable and free countries in the world. A country where you're free to say whatever you like, but not free to kidnap and kill. And I—unlike you—kill only killers."

"You're *all* killers! Every one of you! Tell me about the Pershing and cruise missiles you have hidden all over Western Europe! NATO is nothing but a paid assassin for your great United States of America!"

"We learned that lesson from you and the Japanese," Carter said. "We won't be caught unprepared again. Our defenses will keep the Soviets in line."

"Bah!" Konrad said. "You'll end up killing all of us! And you tell me that *our* methods are out of line!"

Carter's wrist burned. He felt the blood dripping down his hand. The blood was a good sign. It would soak into the ropes and help them grow slack.

"The individual counts," Carter said. "What you and everyone else does adds up to a society. You make your own society corrupt. No one's doing it for you."

"Enough!" Konrad said. "Enough of this talk. Why do you want Bretton?"

"He's an old friend," Carter said and smiled. "Just looking up an old friend."

"Rheinhold?" Konrad said, leering, and stepped back.

Rheinhold jumped forward and belted Carter in the stomach, then kicked Carter's knees. Pain shot through the Killmaster again, drenching him in cold sweat.

"I find it interesting," Carter said, refusing to pant, "that our translation of Wetterfrösche is 'weatherfrog.' You're not good enough to be Weathermen. Just slimy frogs!"

"Who knows about Bretton?" Konrad shouted in the distance. "Please tell us you don't know!"

"Why should anybody care about Bretton?" Carter said, gritting his teeth.

"Karl?" Konrad invited. "Willy?"

The two men stepped forward, alternating blows to Carter's chest and belly. Carter fell against the ropes, glad for their support, as the red-black haze of pain caught him in its uncontrollable grip. Far away he heard moaning. Was it his . . . or the other victim's?

"He's awake again!" one of the men said.

More than hearing it, Carter sensed the movement away from him. The Bulgarian was conscious. Die Wetterfrösche wanted the Bulgarian's information more than they wanted Carter's. Carter allowed himself to rest against the ropes, then he again worked the wrist.

"Nikita, old friend," Konrad said softly. "You must tell us what we want to know so that we can release you."

"But I don't know anything." The Bulgarian's voice was sad, without hope.

"What were your orders?"

"To wait for you in the phone booth on the Königsallee. To follow your directions . . . take the suitcase to you."

"A suitcase full of newspapers!"

"I didn't know . . ."

The sharp cracks of Konrad's hand against the Bulgarian's face echoed in the basement.

"I didn't . . . I didn't . . . I didn't know . . ." the Bulgarian moaned.

Konrad stalked toward Carter, glaring at him, then turned and stalked back toward the Bulgarian.

"All right. I believe you," Konrad said flatly to the Bulgarian.

The Bulgarian sighed, nodded, grateful.

"But don't get your hopes up. What reason do I have now to keep you alive?"

"No, Konrad!" the fat man said.

Konrad whirled to return to Carter.

"Konrad!" the Bulgarian begged in the flickering firelight. "I'll go back to them! Find out whatever you want to know!"

Konrad ignored the fat man as if he were a piece of furniture, a slab of meat.

"We don't play games here, Killmaster," he told Carter. "I want your information now!"

After delivering the message, the cadaverous Wetterfrösche leader spun on his heel, aimed Wilhelmina, and fired. His men watched curiously. Rheinhold held his breath.

Carter flipped Hugo into the palm of his hand.

The Bulgarian's head exploded, bone and cartilage flying into the cold basement hole. The body jerked against the flat planks and ropes.

"So, Killmaster," Konrad said, smiling at the Bulgarian as the stump of head drooped and blew down the cheap clothes. "You see what happens to those who can't help us?"

Carter turned the stiletto upside down and sliced at the ropes that bound his wrist.

"I'm terrified," Carter said.

Konrad rushed at him, his face a mask of cold fury, Wilhelmina raised butt-first to strike.

Suddenly bullets crashed through the room, ricocheting off the stone walls. The man named Willy collapsed, a pool of blood spreading across his belly.

SIX

Bullets sang around Nick Carter and the three remaining Wetterfrösche men. The men crouched, hiding behind the tumbled stones from the walls. They shot up through the ceiling holes and the stairwell at the attackers.

Quickly Carter sawed through the ropes, freed his hand, then went to work on the rest of the ties as ricocheting bullets bit into the wall and planks behind him.

"Where is she?" someone shouted down into the basement. The words were German, but the accent was again Bulgarian.

"You have to pay for her!" Konrad yelled. "We did all the dirty work!"

"We gave you the job in the first place!" another voice shouted from above.

"You broke our agreement!"

"She's ours!"

"Pay or someone else will!"

Again gunfire blasted into and out of the small chamber.

Carter cut himself free. The Bulgarians had traced their "messenger" to the Wetterfrösche hideout. That had been the doomed fat man's unknown mission, not delivering a suitcase full of cash. And now the Bulgarians believed they were close to finding Dr. N. R. Henry, the American scientist—and they intended to have her without paying a single Deutsche mark.

Carter dropped onto his hands and knees, pausing as circulation returned to his limbs and the pounding in his head subsided. He ached all over, but he didn't have time for that.

Two more of the Germans fell—Rheinhold with a bullet through the throat and arm, and a look of horror on his stupid face, and the other man, Karl, bullets riddling his legs and back, turning them into bloody hamburger.

Carter and Konrad were trapped sitting ducks, and Carter knew he wouldn't get out alive to find the scientist if he didn't act quickly.

He slipped Hugo back into his chamois sheath and slid across the ice-cold floor.

Konrad turned, a submachine gun aimed at Carter's head.

"Don't be a fool!" Carter shouted. "Give me my Luger!"

A barrage of bullets suddenly cascaded from above. It was the sign that the Bulgarians would soon rush the basement, an argument for cooperation that Konrad couldn't ignore.

Konrad tossed the Luger to Carter.

"I won't let them take us alive!" he said.

Carter fired at a head peering down the stairwell. The head fell back, a black hole where an eye had been.

"You *are* an idiot," Carter said. "Don't you believe in living for your cause?"

"Causes are to die for!"

"Bullshit! You can't win if you die," Carter said, then shouted to the attackers above in Bulgarian. "We'll tell you where Dr. Henry is if you stop firing!"

There was a sudden, ear-piercing silence.

"Where is s-she?" came a deep voice that stuttered.

Slowly Konrad pivoted. His eyes blazed with fury. He pointed the submachine gun at Carter.

Carter shook his head, disgusted.

"Grow up. I can help you. My government will pay the ransom money. If you want, twice what the Bulgarians promised."

Konrad's face slowly reassembled itself into greed. Greed, fortunately or unfortunately, is one of the most reliable motives for human behavior. It erased from Konrad's memory that both the West German and the United States governments had refused to pay any amount.

"Let us come up," Carter shouted again. "We'll talk."

As voices above consulted, Konrad looked with new interest at Carter.

"It can be done?" he said.

"Anything's possible. You said so yourself."

Konrad looked at the fallen bodies of his dead comrades.

"Perhaps it's not such a bad idea," he said.

"Tell me where she is," Carter suggested, "and we'll figure out a lie they'll believe."

Konrad's eyes narrowed.

"I'm not a fool. That's *my* information. First you pay for it."

Carter shrugged. He needed to get out of this hellhole alive. And if Konrad and his information were with him, all the better.

"What do you say?" Carter shouted to the destroyed building above.

"Very w-well," the stutterer replied. "Drop your guns. Come up with your h-hands raised!"

Carter tucked Wilhelmina inside his jacket in a specially padded pocket designed by AXE that made the gun invisible to any casual viewer. Konrad looked at the weapons scattered around the floor. He picked up a .45 and slid it in the waistband of his jeans. He pulled his heavy jacket over it.

"You'll blow your balls off," Carter said.

Konrad laughed and walked toward the stairs, a swagger in his gait. Flouting danger thrilled him.

Carter followed him up into the icy air.

There were a half-dozen Bulgarians waiting in the night. The only light was the dull glow of the fire in the basement beneath them and the half moon hidden behind overhanging trees. The men's faces were shadows, their dark business suits menacing carbon copies of one another.

"W-where is she?" the stutterer asked, waving a Luger at Carter and Konrad.

"A good German gun," Carter commented.

"You reneged on our deal," Konrad accused the Bulgarian stutterer.

"You stupid swine! T-tell us or you're dead!"

Konrad didn't like the insult. Carter felt him tense, saw the hand slide under the jacket. Carter gave up; Konrad was hopeless. The terrorist would get them both killed.

"I don't deal with double crossers!" Konrad shouted and pulled out the .45.

Carter bent and lunged into the stutterer's stomach.

Konrad shot the .45 at the belly of another Bulgarian. It was the easiest, most certain—and most cowardly—shot.

The Bulgarian went down. Quickly Konrad shot him again.

Carter felt the spray of the dead man's blood on his face. He sped off into the night.

Behind him a hail of the surviving Bulgarians' bullets

finished off the cursing Konrad and his self-limiting dreams.

There was a pause, then shouts.

After a moment of reorganization, the Bulgarians came after Carter. He dodged and ran. The Bulgarians' feet in their sturdy shoes pounded like an army's through the dark rubble of the bombed-out city lot.

At night, all large industrial cities sounded the same. Amid noises of traffic, grinding garbage trucks, distant laughter and music, and the occasional conversations of birds and insects, Carter ran and leaped over the jumbled remains of a half block of buildings not rebuilt since the war. In the distance a siren wailed. It was coming closer. Probably to investigate the gunfire reported by a concerned citizen.

Ahead Carter could see a well-lit street with people strolling unsuspecting to parties or their homes.

Behind, the Bulgarians pursued, silent now except for occasional gunshots and the sounds the men made as they stumbled and ran across the brick and wood litter of destroyed buildings.

Carter raced on, dodging the whining bullets. He was silhouetted by the streetlights ahead, a good target if he'd stop long enough.

It was a loose rock that got him.

A rock that rolled under his flying feet and sent him plummeting down a steep slope into refuse dumped by neighbors too impatient or too cheap to hire haulers.

His shoulder crashed into an old clothes dryer. His feet landed on the springs of a sofa. He rolled behind the dryer, massaged the shoulder, and suddenly felt the pain of his raw wrist.

Above, the Bulgarians talked softly, lining the rim of the dark pit.

Carter opened the door of the dryer, then banged it shut.

"He's d-down there!" the stutterer announced triumphantly.

Bodies slid into the hole.

Carter crept backward on the dirt and debris that sloped gently back up.

"The d-dryer! Try the d-dryer!"

The Bulgarians surrounded the innocent machine, ready to pounce once the door was opened on their quarry. Carter darted away up the dirt slope and into the busy street.

He walked rapidly and slid Wilhelmina into the holster on his back. Three police cars with rotating red lights and wailing sirens passed him, heading for the cellar where they'd find German and Bulgarian corpses and answers to questions they didn't have. With police on the scene, his pursuers would be kept busy avoiding capture themselves.

Carter dusted his suit and straightened the sleeves. He walked along the curb, raised his hand, and with the command of an important West German businessman, hailed a taxi.

The forest green AXE Porsche was where Carter had left it parked. Now it was surrounded by young goggle-eyed boys. They were dressed in the embroidered Bavarian shorts and long socks of mountaineers. They kept their hands in their pockets, good boys well taught by their mothers. Still, their eyes shone with desire. They were singers, probably performing nearby, and they wanted to caress the sleek Porsche.

"Go ahead," Carter told them as he got his keys out. "Do your worst."

The boys stared at him, not sure.

"It's okay," Carter said and grinned. "The wax job is

brand new. You can't hurt it."

As the boys ran their hands over the chrome and paint, Carter got into the car, locked the door, and took out his tiny radio that looked like an ordinary tape player. He put on the earphones, pushed the appropriate buttons, and sat back, waiting for AXE's remarkable satellite electronics to go to work.

Outside the car window, the boys still fondled the exquisite car. They couldn't see Carter because of the tinted window glass, but he watched their pleasure and smiled again. Soon they'd run off to new adventure.

"Well, N3," Hawk's rough voice rumbled in the earphones. "It's about time. What've you got?"

In the distance, Carter heard Hawk snap his butane lighter and drag deeply on one of his ever-present cigars. Carter listened a moment, grinned widely, then told the AXE chief of the events since his last call, and about his capture by Die Wetterfrösche and then by the Bulgarians.

"The Bulgarians don't fit with the information we have," Carter finished. "According to what I heard between the two groups, they must have hired Die Wetterfrösche to do the kidnapping. Any word yet about a missing AWACS?"

"I was waiting for you to ask, N3. Unfortunately, the answer is no. After thorough checking, NATO reports that no AWACS has been even momentarily missing. Are you sure of your identification?"

"It was an AWACS. They're hard to miss."

"I was afraid of that. I think it's unlikely that the Bulgarians built one as a model just to tell Die Wetterfrösche how to set their bombs. Too expensive, and a good bomb artist wouldn't need it."

"Have you thought of sending someone to Bulgaria to investigate?"

"I've considered it, yes," Hawk said.

There was a sudden aloofness in Hawk's voice that told Carter he was about to ask questions whose answers were none of his business.

"Right now the Bulgarian AWACS is an unknown issue," Hawk went on. "Let's drop it. But the Wetterfrösche, that's something else. They've been in frequent contact with the West German government. Their threats are increasing. The kidnapping is turning into blackmail. The terrorists have come to the conclusion that Dr. Henry's information is more important than she is. Either the government pays up, or the gang will put her on drugs, drain her dry of information, and dump her carcass in a river they decline to name."

"They've changed the name of the game."

"Exactly. I trust you're on your way to that address you found for Bretton, N3?"

"Yes, sir."

"It's imperative we get Dr. Henry back, unharmed if possible. If not that, then at least before she talks. I'd hate to lose her, but time is growing short!"

"I understand, sir."

"Good hunting!" Hawk said, his breath exploding as he exhaled a cloud of what Carter knew was vile smoke. "I'm counting on you, N3!"

SEVEN

Nick Carter parked the Porsche a block away from the address he'd found in Ludwig Bretton's employment file. He sauntered down the working-class street of tall brick apartment buildings.

Youths in snap-brim caps stood under streetlights, smoking cigarettes, laughing, and shouting at pretty girls bustling by in winter coats. The traffic had changed and was slower now. The cars were older, many with noisy, smoky mufflers. Families here could afford enough luxuries to not feel underprivileged. But their luxuries were limited to those not of interest to the rich.

More parked old cars lined the street, interspersed with a bakery van, three pickups, a window washer's truck, and assorted beat-up motorcycles. Carter walked past them, looking up at the apartment building that matched Bretton's address. Outside a third-floor window, a man on scaffolding wiped his squeegie with a rag, then polished the glass with a cloth.

Carter climbed the immaculately clean steps. German landlords, like German housewives, scrubbed their steps daily.

Inside, the building smelled of boiled potatoes and

sauerkraut. A baby cried behind one of the first-floor doors. Carter was looking for apartment 3C. He went up two more flights, passing the metallic sounds of televisions, an argument between a husband and wife, and the dank smell of a diaper pail left outside a door for laundry in the morning.

Apartment 3C was at the end of the third-floor hall. A woman in curlers stuck her head out of the doorway of 3A, saw that Carter wasn't whom she was expecting, and ducked quickly back inside.

Carter paused outside 3C and listened. The empty hallway soaked up the sounds of the crowded building and seemed itself full of people. He pressed his ear against the door and heard nothing. He knocked.

The door to 3A opened once more. This time the woman was more hesitant. Carter saw only one eye before the door closed softly.

Carter slipped the toothpick into the old-fashioned door lock and heard the soft clicks as it rearranged the tumblers. He stood to the side and swung the door open into the room.

The apartment was dark, icy from a day or more of no heat. He closed the door, turned on the flashlight that was in the toothpick's case, and scanned the room. Magazines lay open on the low table in front of a battered sofa, left as if their readers would be back at any moment. Three coffee cups were on the table, half full. Bureau and table drawers had been ransacked, clothing, cosmetics, and books strewn on the floor. There was a faint glow from an old floor radio. He walked to it and put his hand on the case. Still warm.

Carter went to the window, opened it, and stuck his head out.

"Cousin Jacques sends you greetings," he said to the window washer.

"*Mon Dieu!*"

"All of ours, actually," Carter said and smiled at the little French pickpocket with the soft round white collar and string bow tie. "Want to come in for a cold cup of coffee?"

The Frenchman sat a moment, then nodded. Carefully he stepped onto the windowsill and into the room.

"The coffee is abominable," the Frenchman said. "I tried it."

"And the radio?"

"Turned it off. The wastrels left it on when they evacuated. Must have been in a hurry." The Frenchman stopped, staring at Carter. "How did you know it had been on?"

"Old sets like this stay lit fifteen minutes or so after they're turned off."

They stared at the radio.

"Not an antique yet," the Frenchman said and pulled on his short auburn goatee. "Just junk. *Très triste*. Very sad."

Carter watched him.

"French secret service?" he asked.

"AXE or CIA?"

The two men laughed and shook hands.

"I wondered when I caught you at the Bohemian," Carter said. "You're a good pickpocket, but it's obviously not your living."

"A little something I learned along the way, *monsieur*," the Frenchman said modestly. "Henri Petit at your service!" The little man clicked his heels together and bowed.

"Nick Carter."

"Ah! The famous Killmaster! I am indeed honored!"

Petit insisted on shaking hands again, then he switched on a lamp while Carter turned on a wall heater. The dim glow from the light showed the room to be Spartan, the furniture worn. It had been a dusty mess even before Petit had searched it.

"Your work?" Carter asked.

"I wanted to be sure," Petit said, nodding. "How did you think to look outside?"

"Housewives and professional window washers know that you can't wash windows at night."

"*Mon Dieu*!" Petit smacked his forehead. "Of course! I found the gear down in the truck and thought it would be the perfect cover to investigate the place." He smiled. "No one else questioned me."

"No one else cared," Carter said, then he took out his cigarette case and opened it for the French agent.

"With pleasure," he said politely and chose one. "Shall we sit and compare notes?"

They went into the kitchen. Carter lit their cigarettes. He sat in a sturdy wooden chair, but Petit rummaged through the cupboards and refrigerator.

"I am hollow!" the little man explained, the cigarette dangling from his lips. "I have this enormous hunger that is inappropriate to my size." He stopped his search to turn, palms upraised beside his shoulders. Smoke curled into his eyes, and he squinted the traditional Frenchman's squint. "Who would think, such a little man with such a big appetite!"

"You burn it off at your work," Carter said, amused.

"That is so," he agreed and turned back to his search, exclaiming as he found eggs, cheese, and a pound of coffee.

"Why did you choose my pockets back at the Bohemian?" Carter asked curiously.

"Ah! A good question," Petit said as he piled food on the counter. "We will have a feast, *n'est-ce pas*?" He poured water from the tap into a chipped enamel pan, then set it on the gas stove to boil. "How do you say? Intuition? Yes, that sounds right. I am not a great agent such as you, Killmaster, but I get along. I rely on the intuition. Sometimes I . . . sense . . . feel . . . get strange ideas. I do not know. When I saw you, something told me you were different. I felt it wise to find out just who you were. The billfold is usually an excellent source."

"And the watch and tie pin?"

"To make it look good. Professional." Petit glanced guiltily at Carter from the corners of his eyes. "You understand?"

"Completely," Carter said and grinned. "And what's more, I don't even mind."

"*Bon*! We shall be friends. And I shall make an omelette feast for my new friend with coffee hot enough to warm our shivering bones!"

The Frenchman took off his jacket, turned it inside out, and tied the arms behind him so that the jacket fell in front like an apron. He looked approvingly at the pile of food on the counter, then dropped the cigarette on the linoleum floor and ground it out with his heel.

He turned to study Carter.

"But first you must do me a favor," he said. "Then we will eat and talk business. My intuition tells me you are very tired. And my eyes tell me someone has beat you on the face and tied your wrists. This was not so when we first met."

"True," Carter admitted.

"A man must feel rested and eager to eat a meal prepared by Henri Claude Renoir Petit, a *great* chef.

Therefore, you must take advantage of the humble bathroom down the short hall off the living room. Bathe, dust your clothes, refresh yourself." The small man shook a finger at Carter. "Do not return until you have. Otherwise my splendid meal will be wasted on a man too tired to properly appreciate it!"

Carter laughed and stood.

"A first-rate idea," he said. "Thanks."

Petit's cheerful whistling of the *Marseillaise* followed Carter down the hall to the bathroom. The grout was coming out and the tile was cracked, and the sink had rust stains that would never wash away, but the bathroom looked like the *salle de bain* of a palace to Carter. He turned on the bathtub's spigots.

He stripped off his clothes, draped them over towel racks, and stood naked before the mirror. His craggy, handsome face was lined with tiredness. Beneath his eyes, deep purple crescents had appeared.

He sighed and stepped into the bathtub. The steam rose and filled his nostrils. He sat in the hot water, then leaned back in the tub, closed his eyes, and let his raw wrist sink into the soothing water.

As he rested, he remembered the monster in the dream he'd had before he'd regained consciousness in the bombed-out Wetterfrösche cellar. Fear. His old friend, the monster to be kept at bay, allowed out only in the safety of the unconscious. He lived with fear constantly. All intelligent men did. The trick was to not let it get out of control.

Carter felt his flesh soften, the muscles relax. The pains in his chest and belly eased. His headache retreated to the edge of consciousness.

Fear was a useful emotion. It kept sane men from doing stupid acts. It helped strengthen men to protect hearth and home. But let out of control, it destroyed individuals and societies. The fire that forged could also destroy.

Carter closed his eyes, put his mind on alert for danger, then allowed himself the luxury of dozing.

The fragrant aroma of fresh coffee awakened him. It reminded him of early winter mornings as a boy. He smiled with memories, stepped out of the tub, and looked in the mirror. Already his face looked refreshed, his rugged features set in relaxed planes and lines.

He toweled off, brushed his hair, and took out an aluminum-foil-covered package from his trousers. He opened it, wrapped the antibiotic cloth around his wrist, and covered it with gauze. With luck, the wounds wouldn't get infected. He dressed slowly, smoothed his clothes, and gargled with warm water.

Again he looked in the mirror. He smiled. Not bad. After a day of tracking, hiding, being beaten, gassed, and shot at, even to himself he looked as if he could step out of a magazine advertisement for adventure. He shook his head, grateful for AXE's stringent training. It paid off in many ways. One of those was in resilience.

In the kitchen, Henri Petit was dishing up omelettes.

"A little beer," he said, gaily twirling the spatula over his head, "a little onion, tomato, and mushrooms—and *violà*!—we have a sauce!" He ladled it over the steaming omelettes and turned. "Well, my Killmaster. You are hungry now, *oui*?"

"Most definitely!" Carter said and sat down at the table.

"At last. An appreciative audience!"

The little Frenchman put the plates on the table, sat, and crossed himself. The two men ate.

"It is not so bad, the beer sauce," Petit said as he

chewed thoughtfully. "There was no wine, of course. Germans drink nothing but beer. Barbarians, but at least the beer is excellent."

"Everything is," Carter said, feeling himself fill with the good food. "Glad you were still hanging around when I got here."

Petit laughed.

"I was just about to leave. I thought to give the apartment a half hour to see if anyone else was drawn to it. I think it was as they left it: no one was here before me. That was a puzzlement since Bulgarians are apparently also after our little group of terrorists."

"Bulgarians?" Carter said. "I wonder why."

Petit's eyes narrowed. Suddenly he chuckled.

"You would not be pulling what you call a fast one, would you, Killmaster? And on a poorly equipped operative like myself?"

Carter laughed.

"All right," he said. "I just found out myself the Bulgarians are interested. Do you know why?"

Henri Petit gave an expressive Gallic shrug.

"Who knows? Russia's henchmen are not notorious for doing anything on their own."

Carter nodded soberly. The men considered the possibility of Soviet involvement.

"And what about at the Bohemian?" Carter said.

"Questions! Questions!" the little man said, rolling his eyes comically. "Now I know your secret weapon. You wear down the innocent with words!" He leaned forward, grinning. "But I will tell you. It is so simple. I was tracking a waiter who works at the Bohemian—Konrad Biberkopf. He was not there, so I came here. One of our agents had reported that he was in Die Wetterfrösche."

"A very thin man, intense, with stooped shoulders?"

"*Oui*! Have you seen him?"

"A couple of hours ago. The Bulgarians killed him."

"Ah. Very sad. But he was a very bad man, so perhaps it is his justice."

"His trail led you here?"

"Just so. And now I am off to Yugoslavia. Care to join me? Perhaps I can teach you about intuition, and you can teach me to be a Killmaster. Not as great as yourself, but at least more skilled than I am?"

"I would be delighted to help in any way I can. But why Yugoslavia?"

"Opatija, a delightful resort on the Yugoslav Riviera."

"The Adriatic coast."

"That's it!" Petit smiled, speared a bite of omelette, and chewed. "This apartment was my last stop. To make sure that the birds had indeed flown. A few years ago my government concluded a secret deal with Die Wetterfrösche in an isolated spot on the coast not far away from Opatija. It seemed to us then that they must have a nest nearby. Today we received a message that one of the gang was seen in the town."

"A good lead," Carter said. "I'll call ahead and have the AXE stringer in Skopje meet us there. Did you find anything else in the apartment to confirm their destination?"

"Nothing. I did learn, however, that Die Wetterfrösche does not keep a tidy house." He raised his hand and shook it. "A pigsty, *mon vieux*! A pigsty!"

Laughing, they finished their meal and Petit poured boiling coffee from the enameled pot into two chipped mugs.

"My government was outraged by the kidnapping of your Dr. Henry," Petit said as he sat back, cradling his cup. "We have our own scientists and high officials who work with NATO. What will happen to them now? We must stop these terrorists who think they can run the world on other people's sweat! That is what I tell myself when I grow discouraged. It is a hard business we've chosen, *n'est-ce pas*?"

"Hard, but when a problem is resolved, a wrong righted, it seems important."

"I sometimes wonder about that. It's the Gallic temperament. It is a world of problems, and we can work on so few."

Carter sipped the coffee. He was warm, relaxed, and well fed. He had information and a good lead. His day had produced interesting results. He was feeling at peace with himself. He smiled.

"That's why we must do the best jobs we can. We set a good example, and hope that more of the world falls into place."

"It is a good hope," Petit said thoughtfully and stroked his neat goatee into a point.

"Thank you for the dinner," Carter said. "It was as excellent as you promised. Now may I offer you something? A ride perhaps, in a very special car to Opatija?"

"Delighted!" the Frenchman said enthusiastically. "I would not relish the trip in the window washer's van!"

"And I will show you some of the new automobile gadgets our AXE scientists have developed."

They raised their coffee mugs in salute, grinned at one another, and drank, looking forward to their nighttime ride.

EIGHT

The morning sun was streaking the sky rose and lavender as Nick Carter and Henri Petit drove at incredible speed through the snow-capped Julian Alps and across the Austrian border into Yugoslavia.

They had entered the republic of Slovenia. In the softly purring Porsche they drove along the winding mountain road that would take them eventually to Opatija. Excellent AXE and French secret service papers had passed them through the sleepy border guards' nonchalant examinations. Now relaxed, they admired the beautiful morning. Sheep grazed on the mountain slopes. Early-rising farmers were out in slouched hats, tending animals on small farms nestled in valleys.

The day would be bright and clear, a good day to look for information in one of the most unusual nations in the world.

"Do you know what Yugoslavs say about their country?" Carter asked Petit as they drove through the velvet-covered mountains.

"No, *mon vieux*. What is that?"

"They say they're one country with two alphabets,

three religions, four languages, five peoples, six republics, seven borders, and twenty million different opinions on every issue."

Petit slapped his knee, and the two agents laughed.

"Now you must show me the devices you told me about," the Frenchman said. "The sun is up, the day is good, and I am properly in the mood."

"Push that button," Carter suggested.

Petit looked at the red button in the walnut dashboard.

"What will happen?" he asked suspiciously.

"You won't know unless you try."

"A challenge! Very well . . ."

The Frenchman pressed his thumb down on the button. Instantly a five-inch-wide translucent rectangle appeared on the walnut dashboard. Two columns of words were arranged on the screen. Beside each word was a small square glowing silver.

"I am baffled," Petit said, leaning forward to study it. "Explain, please." He reached out his hand.

"Better not touch it," Carter warned. "This car is run by a microcomputer system. For instance, when I lock the doors, they *really* are locked. No one can get in except me. My key not only has special notches to indicate it's mine, but it's also electronically sensitized to my system. If someone else picks up the key and tries to unlock the door, the computer knows it's not me because the key will instantly integrate the physical body rhythms of the new person. The car won't allow itself to be unlocked. Once I have the key again, it will work perfectly."

"Very ingenious! American know-how at work, yes?" The Frenchman stroked his goatee. "And this amazing panel here. What does it do?"

"It's part of the computer system. Each of those words

is a command. All you have to do is touch one of them—anywhere on the word itself or the silver square next to it—and you get immediate action."

"I am intrigued. What kind of great action is possible?"

"Well, if you were to touch 'Spike,' little explosives that look like nails would scatter from the back of the car. The spikes explode when they're crushed by very heavy weight. Any vehicle chasing me would lose its tires."

"Amazing. One better than the old nail trick. It never did work well, did it? A few punctures, the nails stick in the tires, and twenty miles away the hooligans are still after you!"

"Exactly. And those words, 'Port' and 'Starboard,' refer to submachine guns mounted above the tires. The fenders retract, the guns come out, and four bull's-eyes appear on the dash so that I can aim and fire. Or I can simply turn on the computer intelligence, and it will fire for me when the target's in the hairlines."

Petit sat back, staring at Carter.

"I am truly without words. These 'gadgets,' as you call them, are unlike anything we have. I do not think we have anything approaching this yet."

"You will. My favorite of all is 'Escape.' Do you ever watch James Bond movies?"

"No, no. They are much too silly for me."

"When you missed his car with the front seat that blasts up and out when he needs to escape the villains. It has rockets so he can jet away."

"How can you stand such absurdity? A 007 movie!"

Carter laughed as the French agent tugged angrily on his goatee.

"They're like reading newspaper comics. Lighthearted entertainment. Amusing."

"Amusing! They mock the hard, dangerous work we do!"

"Perhaps, but I always leave laughing, and that's not to be underrated these days."

"No, I suppose not," Petit said slowly. "Very well, I must admit I like the Folies Bergère. The tone is different, but the results are the same."

"We agree in our own fashion."

"Yes. And now about 'Escape'?"

"Imagine it. You're driving ninety, and you know you can push this wonderful machine easily up to a hundred and twenty. You're not worried by the car chasing you. Suddenly, out of nowhere, two more cars appear ahead of you. You're trapped. What do you do?"

"Pray." Petit crossed himself.

"You hit 'Escape.' All the computer functions go into action. It literally takes over defense. It covers you for three hundred and sixty degrees around—handles any vehicle that moves. It can use guns, smoke, nails, and special shock absorbers. Turbo jets that give you three-hundred-mile-an-hour bursts of speed. You've got an army at your disposal to eliminate attackers and make your escape certain."

"I hesitate to ask, but is the car also bulletproof?"

"Of course. Nearly bombproof, too."

Petit sighed.

"What can I say, Killmaster from AXE? Just looking at that screen makes me nervous. The potential! One must be very intelligent to be the master of such resources."

Carter pressed the red button again, and the screen disappeared.

"It's not difficult," he said. "Remember how hard it was when you first learned to drive? It seemed as if there were a thousand things to remember at once. Running a computer—or a computerized car—is much the same. Quickly the impossible becomes not only possible, but a pleasure."

"I think I will take your word for it, Nick Carter." The Frenchman held up his hands, then turned them. "These hands were made to caress women, not machines!" He cupped the hands over his chest and grinned. "Real women with *big* bazookas, as you say in your country. This I know and approve of!"

The men laughed again, and the morning passed quickly with talk and scenery as the road wound down through the mountains and crossed from Yugoslavia's Slovenian republic to the Croatian. Far off between the peaks, they caught occasional glimpses of the sapphire blue Adriatic, glistening in the sun.

The stark countryside they drove through was beautiful, all of it worthy of any picture post card. But the soil was only a few inches deep in most places. It was rough going for the farmers who dotted the landscape with truck gardens and brown, fallow fields.

When they at last pulled into Opatija, they were met with clean streets and buildings, tourists with cameras, and the sea that freshened the air and gave a nautical atmosphere to the resort.

It was a small town, only thirteen thousand people, and Carter quickly found the Hotel Ambassador. With its two hundred rooms and visiting throngs, it would be a safe place for two more tired tourists to rest. They would sleep a few hours first, then get to the business of finding whether Die Wetterfrösche had brought Dr. Henry there.

Carter and Petit had top-floor corner rooms at the Ambassador Hotel. They sat outside Carter's room on the fifty-foot-long wraparound balcony in the warm afternoon sun.

From their small table they admired the glassy harbor bobbing with small craft. A two-masted schooner sailed out into the shimmering sea, probably taking tourists to a relaxed dinner where they would be served by white-coated waiters in sailors' berets.

"You will go see your stringer?" Petit said. His face had relaxed, and his gray eyes danced with renewed enthusiasm for life.

The men ate a meal of *djuvec*, a spicy dish of tomatoes, peppers, rice, chopped meat, and grated cheese.

"Yes," Carter said, "Alex Markov. He's arrived."

After the two agents' long drive and some rest on the old hotel's firm beds, they were again ravenous. Food was one of the world's great pleasures and solaces, Carter reflected. The men ate hungrily as they looked out across the picturesque harbor.

"It's not Paris," Petit said as he dabbed his goatee with a cloth napkin, "but it has its own charm, yes?"

"There's a fishing village south of here that reminds me of Portofino," Carter said and drank from his glass of local wine.

Yugoslavia was one of the great wine-producing countries of Europe, but few people elsewhere knew that. Local wines were seldom transported out of their regions.

"Ah, the fishing villages. I remember as a boy going in the summer with my mother to Cannes. It was just after the war. We had no money, so we hitchhiked. Everyone did in those days. GIs would give us rides and Hershey bars. When we got to Cannes, we would lie on the beach and watch the clouds. My mother would tell me stories of what it was like before."

"And your father?"

"Dead," the Frenchman said, his facial lines suddenly downturned with sadness. "The infantry." He smiled briefly. "He was an architect. He said in the infantry he would get to see a lot of buildings firsthand, and he wouldn't have to bomb them. That pleased him."

"I'm sorry he was killed," Carter said.

"I, too, but that is life, *n'est-ce pas*? He was a Communist, and I am a Catholic. Still, we both chose the infantry. I see a lot of buildings in my work."

Carter smiled.

"I never looked at it that way," he said.

"A very important distinction. We kill individuals, and not for the joy of it. We do not eliminate masses of people, cultures, races. Only the odd ones who try to destroy our ways of living."

"Is that why you became an agent?"

Petit shrugged.

"Who knows?" he said. "My mother says it is because I, in the true French tradition, am a romantic."

"And you don't really come from a family of scofflaws."

"A good expression, yes? I liked that expression very much!" The Frenchman beamed and ate. "I think I would have liked to come from a long line of scofflaws!"

The voice was small and tinny, shouting up from below in Serbo-Croatian.

"Mister! Oh, mister! You want a guide?"

Carter and Petit leaned over the railing. In the street stood a boy about twelve years old, dressed in tattered cut-off trousers and a clean shirt.

The boy waved enthusiastically up at them.

"I am a good guide, mister! Take you anywhere you want. We love Americans here!"

Carter pulled some coins from his pocket.

"An excellent idea, Killmaster," Petit said and smiled. "I will join you."

"Sorry, friend!" Carter called down. "Some other time!"

The agents tossed the coins to the boy. He clapped his hands and bent to gather them.

"This is good food, too soon gone," Petit said as he settled back in his chair.

A waiter appeared, took away their plates, and brought two cups of steaming Viennese coffee.

"I think that while you are visiting your stringer," the Frenchman went on, his eyes on the retreating back of the waiter, "I shall make a few calls, see what I can learn."

"Good. I'll be back as soon as I can."

Carter drained his cup and stood up as the boy from the street ran along the balcony to their table.

Carter sat down again, looking at the urchin.

The boy stood with the coins spread flat on the palms of both hands. He held them up. His eyes shone.

"I will take you everywhere," the boy said. "*Everywhere*!"

The Frenchman laughed.

"You don't understand, *mon ami*," he said.

"Those are a gift," Carter explained gently. "We don't need a guide."

The boy's head drooped. He slid the coins off his palms and onto the table.

"Then I haven't earned them," he said and turned to go.

"Wait," Carter said. "A misunderstanding. Perhaps you can do something else for us."

"An excellent idea," Petit approved.

"We are looking for someone," Carter said.

"Anyone! Anything!" the boy said excitedly, his eyes once more on the coins that could now be his.

"A gray-haired woman," Carter said. "An American in her fifties. She's with a group of Germans. One of the Germans is named Ludwig Bretton, a big tall man who plays the accordian."

The boy scooped the coins off the table and dropped them inside his pants pocket. He patted the pocket.

"If she is here, I will find her!" the boy vowed and ran off.

"You are a good man, Nick Carter," Petit said, smiling quizzically.

"Don't let it get around," Carter said and stood again. "I'll keep in touch."

He walked back into his room, down the hall and stairs, and through the lobby into the oldest of Yugoslavia's coastal resorts, Opatija. He wore sunglasses and loose tourist clothes.

Small shops and cafés lined the streets. To the south were Italian-style villas with red tile roofs, reminders that Opatija had once belonged to Italy until reallocation after World War II. The Italians had a long-standing influence, dating back to the fifteenth century when Venetians ruled the area.

Carter walked among the jostling crowds. The women swung straw purses, and the men wore shorts and cameras dangling around their necks. Record players sang with Croatian folk songs. Outdoor café tables were filled with tired tourists sipping coffee, mineral water, and cocktails. It was off-season in Opatija, but from the large number of intrepid visitors, no guidebook would bother to announce it.

Carter found the address Markov had given him, a small pension of clapboard and brick, set back from the street behind a low wooden fence.

He went in, down a narrow hallway that smelled of cooking lamb and onions. The door was ajar. It shouldn't have been ajar. There was movement, rustling inside the room.

He stood back, took a deep breath, and swung open the door. On the other side of the stringer's rented room another door closed softly.

Quickly Carter slipped inside and closed the door behind him.

In an old-fashioned whitewashed sleeping room of lace and cotton, Alexander Markov, the AXE stringer from Skopje, a twenty-six-year-old helicopter pilot with no known family, sat slumped in a chair, a knife buried to the hilt in his heart.

NINE

Nick Carter stopped only long enough to feel for a pulse in Alexander Markov's throat. Blood soaked the AXE stringer's white shirt and drained down to his khaki trousers. The young man was dead, but the flesh was hot with the memory of life.

Carter raced out the door that he'd heard close, down an alleyway, and into a quiet street rimmed overhead with windowboxes and potted plants.

He looked up and down the street. The edge of a woman's skirt gaily decorated with yellow and blue flowers showed briefly as she swept away around a corner.

He followed her swiftly into the tourist-crowded street on which Markov's pension faced. The woman wove through the families and couples, her pace brisk, trying to look casual.

Even with only her back to him, Carter recognized her.

It was Vera Georgiev, the black hair she'd worn braided and coiled on her head in the Pirin Mountains now cascading to her waist. Her gait was strong and certain, the straight legs swinging to a rhythm that came like music to those who loved walking. Men turned and stared at her. Haughty as a queen she paced on.

Carter slowed, following her. She was a Macedonian agent, and the evidence indicated she'd killed young Markov.

As she turned toward Opatija's bay, there was a new tenseness to her shoulders. Her head cocked slightly as if listening. She never looked over her shoulder, but she knew she was being followed.

Casually, Carter crossed the street and let the distance between them lengthen.

But it wasn't his presence that was disturbing Vera Georgiev. A woman was also following Vera, too closely and without any understanding of secretive grace.

Vera strode on, downhill toward the fish markets and stores above the stone-ledged bay. The woman who followed her was short and slight, brown-haired, with hands that seemed to pull at the air in front of her to drag her one determined step after another.

Vera mingled in a crowd of multilingual visitors gathered around a painter and canvas. The woman following her pushed into the throng too. Carter stood back, leaning against a shady tree, relaxed.

Vera ducked inside a nearby nautical store for tourists. The other woman stopped outside and faced the artist who talked while he painted. But her eyes were on the doorway, waiting for Vera.

Carter smiled and walked around the throng toward the back of the shop, along a rock ledge above the sea where bikini-clad sunworshippers lay glistening with oil.

Ahead, a young woman with small breasts and long legs stood up abruptly, walked to the edge, and arced into the bay. She came up waving and shouting for her friends to join her. Three of them ran to the edge and jumped into the bay's water, rippling without surf because of the many islands that sheltered it.

Vera came out the back of the nautical store and ran up the street, away from the woman who had unsuccessfully tailed her.

Again Carter followed the Macedonian agent.

She slowed to angle north past shops displaying filigreed jewelry, pottery, and woodcarvings. Carter watched her movements and fell back even farther. There was still intent to her gait, but her shoulders were relaxed. She was concentrating on her destination.

At last she swung into a small bookstore with a window display of books on Alexander the Great, born and bred in Macedonia. A doorbell tinkled as she entered.

Carter walked casually by and saw her talking with the shopkeeper behind the counter. The AXE agent stopped at a newsstand, bought a paper, and returned to again pass the window. Vera was nowhere in sight.

Carter raced around the shop and down an alley. The store's back door was firmly closed, and because the street along the back was a dead end, she would have had to pass Carter to leave.

He returned to the front of the store, took off his sunglasses and put on a pair of rimless glasses, slouched his shoulders, and walked in.

"May I help you, sir?"

The shopkeeper was a small man with bright brown eyes that looked steadily into the distance.

"I would like a book on Macedonian history," Carter said, his voice high and fussy. "An entertaining book, you know, to spend a night alone with."

"Very good, sir. I think I have just the one for you."

Carter followed the small man as he walked to a shelf and scanned the titles.

"Did you happen to notice that beautiful lady who just came into your establishment?" Carter said, smoothing his hair. "I believe she's Macedonian herself. I do want to learn all I can."

Politely ignoring Carter, the shopkeeper took down a dusty book. The section of shelves was covered with various books on Macedonia—novels, history, politics, geography, language—a collection put together by someone who'd chosen Macedonia as the shelves' subject, not by the individual titles, authors, or areas of study.

"Here you are," the small man said. "Secondhand, I'm afraid. But a classic. You do read Greek, don't you?"

"Of course," Carter said. "Ring it up, will you? I'll just use your rest room to wash my hands."

"Sir!"

Carter skirted the counter and walked along a dark narrow hallway, the proprietor in fast pursuit. Carter opened a door into a storage area. Empty.

"Please, sir! I must insist!"

A second door proved to be the lavatory. Empty, too. And then the front door opened and tinkled shut.

Carter brushed past the proprietor and back into the store. A plump woman with bundles in her arms walked toward the stacks of books.

Carter raced again toward the back door and looked out. The alley was empty. Then he knew. When the plump woman had come into the store, Vera must have slipped out. She would run and be out of sight by now. Carter smiled. She was a good agent. Then he frowned. She was capable of killing Markov.

Carter smoothed his clothes and adjusted his glasses.

"How much did you say the book was?" he asked the shopkeeper.

The man took a deep breath, wiped the sweat off his brow, and told him.

Carter dropped the dinars on the counter, picked up the

book, and thanked the shopkeeper politely.

"If that beautiful young woman comes back," he said, "please tell her Nikola was here. She can find me at the Ambassador Hotel."

Carter left in the hazy golden sunshine that precedes sunset in Opatija. He took off the rimless glasses and tucked the book wrapped in brown paper under his arm. He strolled back toward the hotel.

The crowds had thinned, returning to their villas and hotels to bathe and rest for leisurely dinners over candlelight and wine.

But there was a crowd in front of the Ambassador Hotel. An old ambulance was parked at the curb, its back doors wide open.

Attendants in white coats and sterile masks carried out a stretcher. The prone figure on the stretcher was completely covered with a sheet. The crowd watching talked in awed, hushed voices. Carter heard one person say "heart attack," and then another answered cockily "too much drink or sex." They laughed, the living crowing over the dead, as the siren wailed away through the dusk.

Carter strolled through the lobby. A quick heart attack was perhaps a good way to die. Still, he wouldn't wish it on anybody.

The thought that came next was perhaps intuition, and that might have been what made him think it in the first place. He strode to the registration desk.

"Who was on that stretcher?" he demanded from the clerk behind the counter.

"What?" The clerk was sweating. A dead man in the hotel wasn't good for business.

"Was that Henri Petit?" Carter asked.

The man stared at Carter miserably.

"Yes, sir. I'm afraid it was. A tragedy of monumental proportions. And in my hotel!"

Carter slapped his hands on the reception desk. The hotel man jumped and looked at Carter glumly.

"Fortunately, no one knew him, sir," he said. "It was an accident. I'm sure your stay here will be pleasant and uneventful."

Carter turned on his heel and walked away.

"Believe me! The hotel had nothing to do with it! Our guests are the most relaxed and happy of all in Opatija!"

Carter turned again. Henri Petit couldn't be dead.

"Where did they take him?" Carter asked coldly.

"Mr. Petit? The hospital . . . the morgue . . . I don't know, sir. Does it matter?"

In his mind, Carter once again saw the clowning Frenchman preparing omelettes in the slovenly Wetterfrösche apartment in Düsseldorf. He saw the delighted little man explore the possibilities of the AXE-modified Porsche. He heard his voice as he generously threw coins down to the Opatija boy.

"It matters to me," Carter said.

The hotel man stared at Carter. Sweat drenched his face.

"Very well," he said at last. "I'll see what I can find out."

He picked up the telephone, and Carter returned to the reception desk to listen and wait.

A tug at his sleeve interrupted his frustration.

Carter looked down as the clerk's voice droned on the telephone.

"I've found them," the Opatija boy from the balcony said.

Carter frowned.

"The American woman," the boy said, then backed off a step, uncertain. "The Germans . . . I thought you . . ."

Carter put a hand on the boy's shoulder and looked at the desk clerk.

"I'll be back," he told him. "I'll expect the information then."

The hotel man nodded gloomily and spoke again into the receiver.

"Where are they?" Carter asked the boy.

"I'll show you," he said and scampered toward the lobby door.

Carter met him there, and the two walked briskly into the coastal resort's twilight, along the lantern-lit street, past the cafés and stores, south on Highway 2 skirting the bay that stretched to Rijeka. Other tourists were out for predinner strolls, and the man and his guide picked up their pace.

"Do you like my town?" the boy asked as they passed a couple holding hands. "It's a good town, don't you think?"

"Very beautiful," Carter replied. "But it's large enough that a young boy would have a hard time finding one person."

"Many tourists," the boy agreed. "But one of my uncles is the postman and an aunt works in a beauty shop. My cousins clean streets and run errands." He smiled. "It's our Opatija."

"I see," Carter said and smiled. "You must be alone in the world then."

The boy had thin hair that fell into his eyes. Light from a new moon shone on freckles and a nose that would someday have a handsome bump. His face was solemn and resigned.

"They're gone many years, my parents. A fishing accident."

"I'm sorry," Carter said.

The boy shrugged.

"I live with my mother's sister."

"The beauty shop aunt?"

"Together we do fine," the boy said and smiled. "She has red hair like fire. All out of a bottle!"

"You have fun together."

"But I've always wanted to go to the great United States of America. Is it good there?"

"We like it."

"Someday I'll have enough money, and my aunt and I will go together!"

They left the highway and climbed a narrow path up a steep incline. Above were foothills dark and forbidding with night.

"The driveway is over there," the boy said and gestured to the right. "This way is quicker."

"Any other houses around?"

"A few. But not close together. Vacation places. They're empty a lot because the owners don't live here."

"I see," Carter said, reaching into his pocket. "I want to surprise my friend. Here." He pressed bills into the boy's hand. "This will give you a start toward the United States."

The boy held up the money and stared at it in the moonlight.

"So much!" he exclaimed. "I did that good a job?"

"Better than you'll ever know," Carter said. "Now go back to town and send the police. Tell them a U.S. agent is here and that Die Wetterfrösche—can you say Die Wetterfrösche?"

His eyes round as saucers, the boy repeated the terrorist gang's name.

"Good. Tell them Die Wetterfrösche has a hideout and give them directions. I'll probably still be here, but maybe not. Think you can remember all that?"

"Yes, sir!" The boy licked lips suddenly dry with nervous excitement.

"You're a smart boy and a very good guide. Now run!"

Carter clapped him on the back.

The boy tore down the path, his slight body blending with bushes and trees until at last he disappeared around a curve.

Carter turned up the path and climbed. Through the trees ahead dim house lights glowed. He slowed, listening to the nighttime songs of birds and insects. There would have to be lookouts posted. Die Wetterfrösche was too smart to be unprotected.

He heard a twig snap off the path ahead. The acrid smell of cigarette smoke wafted faintly down the hill.

He moved carefully, walking softly. Leafy branches brushed his face and clothes.

The sentry was in a stand of pines, sheltered under their broad branches as if he were another tree. Across his arms he balanced an AK-47.

Carter slipped off the path, feeling ahead with his feet one step at a time. In the distance a jay suddenly screeched and fluttered away.

The sentry turned, and another jay called gaily.

Carter crept forward.

Six feet away, the sentry dropped his cigarette into the duff and ground it out.

Carter lunged.

The sentry swiveled.

Carter wrapped an arm around the sentry's neck and

jerked him back. The AK-47 plopped into the duff.

Gasping, the sentry tore at Carter's arm, then rammed an elbow back into Carter's belly. He'd been trained well.

Carter jerked again, feeling his muscles ripple with tension and movement.

The sentry thrashed and went limp, unconscious.

Carter lowered him to the ground.

He unknotted the man's handkerchief from his neck and stuffed it into his mouth. He took a handkerchief from his own pocket and tied the gag in place. Next he took off the man's belt, and strapped and buckled it around his legs. He pulled a small package of special striated nylon rope the size of twine from his pocket. He cut off a length, rolled the sentry over, and tied his hands behind his back. The man wouldn't warn anyone of Carter's presence.

The Killmaster dragged him from his lookout spot and rolled him under a thick-trunked tree. The smell of disturbed pine needles filled the air.

"Joachim!" the voice called softly through the trees. It was another sentry. "Joachim! Where are you? Let's have a smoke!"

Carter crouched, ready.

"Joachim!" the voice called again. An edge of worry had crept in.

The footsteps were stealthy. Carter balanced the rest of the striated rope in his hands. The new man wouldn't be as easy.

"This isn't funny, Joachim!" Now there was anger. "Ludwig said . . ."

Carter tied the rope to the trunk of the tree beside him. He crawled across to another tree five feet away. He pulled the rope taut and anchored it to the second tree's trunk.

The footsteps stopped. The sentry had suddenly

realized that his companion in the forest might not be Joachim.

Silently, Carter returned to the first tree.

Not far away, branches softly batted against something hard. Now the feet moved with the savvy of a man who knew how to tread. The feet padded in a wide circle, slowly closing in on Joachim's sentry post.

Carter felt in the duff by his feet, found a pinecone, then found two more.

Slowly, inexorably the feet closed in.

At last, when the sentry was off to Carter's left, about twelve feet from Joachim's post, the Killmaster stood silently.

He lobbed one cone ten feet, another fifteen feet, and the last twenty feet in a straight line of possible escape.

The sentry lunged after his retreating foe, his feet no longer light but heavy with pursuit. He ran past Carter, between the pines.

The toe of his boot caught on the rope. He pitched forward, a muffled yell cut off as his face hit the duff.

Carter pounced.

The man rolled, savagely whipping the butt of his AK-47 at Carter's head.

Carter dodged. Slashed the gun away. Jumped onto the sentry's heaving chest.

The sentry belted his fist into Carter's face.

Carter's ears rang. He shook his head. Blood dripped from his nose.

Again the sentry swung his fist.

Carter caught it in midair and stared down at the shadowed face beneath him.

The sentry's lips curled, his teeth gleaming ivory in the forest night.

The two fighters froze that way for a moment in a

contest of strength and determination.

Sweating, Carter slowly forced the man's fist back. The sentry's cheeks shuddered with effort.

"Who . . . are . . . you . . . ?" he grunted.

"A friend like you," Carter said softly.

He bashed his other fist into the sentry's jaw.

The man's eyes rolled. He went limp.

Carter gagged and tied him, and left him fourteen feet away from his companion Joachim, hidden under a tree where the two men couldn't help one another to escape.

Once again Carter prowled up the hill, still listening. Ahead he heard the scratchy voice of a radio announcer coming faintly from the house. He crossed a dirt driveway to the two-story structure and slipped into the deep shadows of more trees.

He surveyed the area. The house was a board and batten cottage with an open-air porch. Steps ran down on the two sides that Carter could see. A dirt path wound around the cottage, weeds and grasses growing tall on both sides. No attempt at landscaping had been made. The building was nestled among pines, all the windows alight. From where Carter stood the light was bright, but at any distance it would dim, lost among the thick trees. From the highway below, it would be invisible. On the second floor, shadows moved behind curtained windows.

Silently Carter crept forward. The wooden porch would creak, so he stayed on the dirt path.

Through a large picture window he could see two men and two women sitting at an old felt-covered table in the living room. They played cards, and one of the women was the one who'd unsuccessfully tailed Vera Georgiev in Opatija. She stood up now, as grim as she'd been when Carter had first seen her. She went to the radio and turned up the volume.

It was a news report, relaying in German that the violent gang Wetterfrösche was still at large and demanding the release of nineteen of their fellow terrorists plus a ransom of a million Deutsche marks.

The woman patted the radio affectionately, and the four gang members laughed.

Silently, Carter moved on past a corner of the living room where three men drank beer from bottles and talked intently.

The next window was translucent and small, probably a bathroom.

The third window showed a gray-haired woman alone, tied to a straight-backed wooden chair.

Her head slumped forward with either unconsciousness or exhaustion. She wore a torn silk blouse, a long dinner skirt, and pumps. Carter took a deep breath. He'd found Dr. N. R. Henry.

Then he heard it. The movement of many feet in the forest. They were trying to be quiet, but there were too many of them. It was too soon for the police, Carter thought. Then who . . .?

Carter faded back, his eyes on Dr. Henry. She remained silent and still, immobilized in another world.

The feet ran, pounding.

Carter slipped in among the thick branches of a pine tree. He melted into the dark shadows and pulled Wilhelmina from the small of his back.

"L-Left!" a harsh voice shouted. "You there, r-right! Around the corner! G-go in the back!"

Carter crouched. It was the Bulgarians!

Gunfire exploded, rocking the quiet of the pristine mountainside. Flashes of red-streaking bullets lit the night as they bit into the cottage.

TEN

Nick Carter raced forward and hurled himself over the porch's railing and through the glass window of the room where Dr. Henry was tied.

Window glass shattered, spraying into the room as Carter crashed in. Dr. Henry slowly raised her head, tried to focus her eyes, then slumped once more.

Carter rubbed his shoulder and padded forward as the Wetterfrösche safe house rocked with shouts, screams, and gunfire.

He flipped out Hugo and sliced the American scientist's bonds. She fell forward into his arms. She was small and light, her face bruised, one eye blackened.

Feet thundered through the house. Stray bullets shot through the walls into the small room where Dr. Henry had been held captive.

Carter carried her to the window and kicked out more glass shards.

Loud thumping came from the closet next to the window. The door crashed and bowed as if someone were ramming his shoulder into it.

"Blasted door!" the voice inside shouted in French. "Intractable door!"

Again the door thundered and bowed.

"Henri!"

Carter turned the handle. Locked.

"*Mon vieux!* Is that you?"

"Hold on!"

Carter ran back to the chair and lay the doctor across it. Quickly he slipped out the toothpick and unlocked the door, and Henri Petit barreled out.

The Frenchman wrapped his arms around Carter's chest and danced him around the room over the crackling glass.

"My Killmaster to the rescue!"

"Come on, Henri! We've got to get out of here!"

Once more he picked up the doctor as Petit scrambled out the window.

"I thought you were dead," Carter said as he crawled out.

"Never!" the Frenchman said from the porch. "My mother wouldn't allow it!"

"Watch out," Carter warned as the little man stood exposed. "Germans and Bulgarians are everywhere."

Petit cocked his head, listening as the gunfire lessened and the crashing sounds of one-to-one combat rattled in the old house. Nimbly he leaped over the rail.

"Hand her down, my friend."

Carter passed the doctor over the railing.

"Bulgarians, too? The damned Germans caught me in the hotel room and knocked me out with some drug. They've got an ambulance. Must've brought it all the way from Germany. A good cover, yes?"

"Very good, unfortunately," Carter said as he vaulted the rail. "There's a path through the trees. Follow me."

Petit handed the doctor once more to Carter, and Carter led the Frenchman through the trees as the house grew quiet, then exploded with Bulgarian shouts.

"Sounds like the Germans lost," Petit said.

"The Bulgarians will be looking for the doctor now."

Carter paused to move the woman from his arms to his shoulder.

"Not a very elegant way for an important scientist to ride," Petit observed.

Carter chuckled, and the two men moved rapidly through the trees. The forest birds and animals were quiet, still in shock from the violent invasion of their solitude. The sea wind swept the treetops, and the men moved at last onto the dirt trail.

Suddenly Carter felt a hand on his shoulder.

"Stop," Petit whispered in his ear. He squeezed Carter's shoulder reassuringly and dropped the hand. "Someone ahead. A Bulgarian perhaps, guarding their flanks."

"I didn't hear anything," Carter said. "Are you sure?"

Petit nodded and pulled on his goatee.

"The intuition," he whispered. "Be right back."

As the small man darted off, Carter faded into the trees. He checked his watch.

A furry forest animal scurried in the duff, sent up a dust cloud, and disappeared down a hole. Distantly, a bird sang, then two and three. They were hesitant calls for the hillside to return to normalcy.

Carter shifted the doctor's weight onto the other shoulder. Above the trees the sky was black, the crescent of the new moon showing in a gap between branches.

In her sleep, the woman shivered, and Carter realized the night was growing brittle with cold. He turned. The house's lights showed faint through the trees. Again he checked his watch. Petit was gone a long time.

Carter moved his feet and flexed his legs. The cold could stiffen him. He still wore only the loose tourist shirt and trousers. The woman on his shoulder moaned softly.

"Where am I?" she said feebly.

He stood her on his feet.

"Nick Carter, ma'am," he told her. "From the United States. You're in Yugoslavia."

She shook her head as if to clear it, and he braced her as she lost her balance.

"I'm cold," she announced, still not comprehending.

"I know. I'll get you out of here as quickly as I can."

She jerked her head up.

"The terrorists!"

"You're safe for the moment." He rubbed her arms. "Move around," he suggested. "It'll help to warm you."

She lifted her feet slowly, put them down, then shuddered. Her teeth chattered.

Again Carter looked at his watch. The Frenchman had been gone too long, but he couldn't leave the doctor to find him.

"Can you walk?" he asked her.

"I think so," she said, looking at him with the wondering eyes of a child. "I didn't tell them anything." The eyes narrowed. "I must get back to Geilenkirchen," she decided. "Check my jet. That's in West Germany, you know. NATO."

"I know. Come on."

He took her arm and urged her down the trail.

"We have to be quiet," he told her. "There may be Bulgarians around."

"Bulgarians? What are they doing here?"

"Please, Dr. Henry. Quiet."

"What do the Bulgarians want with me?" Her voice rose and she stopped dead in the trail.

"The same thing that Die Wetterfrösche wants, I imagine. Now let's get out of here!"

He half led and half dragged her down the path. She plodded along, her feet not yet coordinated with her mind. He supported her as she occasionally tripped on the roots of trees hidden by the night.

"That's it," she suddenly announced and sat down on the trail.

"Okay."

He picked her up, annoyed by her obstinacy. Then she screamed.

The hand that came out of the forest was swift and perfectly aimed. It struck the side of Carter's neck.

He fell to his knees, and Dr. Henry rolled away.

The next blow was to his skull with something hard. Hard like the butt of a rifle. Black clouds crowded his mind. His head split open and filled with a pain-filled void. He closed his eyes, lost to unconsciousness.

ELEVEN

Cool water bathed Nick Carter's face. Cool water and a soft cloth wielded by a gentle hand. Pain swelled his head into a woolly balloon, but the room was warm, the water refreshing. Slowly he felt the pain fade to a throb.

"He's the one," the boy's voice said.

Carter opened his eyes. He was in the living room of the Wetterfrösche safe house. The card table was tipped over and ripped with bullets. Six bodies—the German terrorists—lay sprawled throughout the room, their AK-47s beside them. One of them was the small dark woman who had tailed Vera Georgiev. A few local policemen, probably all the police the small town had, moved about the bodies, silently picking up guns and gathering evidence.

"He's the one who sent me," the Opatija boy went on, his freckled face tight and scared. "Will he be all right?"

"I count thirteen bodies, sir," one of the policemen said as he entered the room. "Two upstairs. I've found one alive, but he's wounded pretty bad."

The policeman who sat in front of Carter nodded grimly.

"You feel well enough to talk?" he asked Carter.

"Sure."

The policeman waved away the man who'd been bathing Carter's face. The bather was the oldest there, a stout man with a jolly red face now lined with shock. This sort of thing didn't happen in Opatija, his jerky movements seemed to say as he picked up the basin of water and walked out of the room.

"Let's have it," said the sturdy policeman sitting in front of Carter.

His head still pulsing with pain, Carter told him how he'd trailed Die Wetterfrösche from West Germany to the Opatija cottage, that the kidnapped American scientist had been with them, and that it had probably been a Bulgarian sentry who had knocked Carter out while he was distracted by the woman doctor.

"So there's a French agent missing, too?"

Carter nodded. "There's not much you can do here. They're probably on their way to Sofia. They may be government agents."

"What makes you think so?"

"The way they acted. Professionals."

The police chief looked thoughtfully at Carter.

"Yes. The Bulgarian government. That is a problem," he said at last, then called to the policeman standing in the door. "I want to see the survivor. Where is he?"

Carter stood to follow the chief and saw the staring eyes of the boy.

"You've been a big help," he told him. "Thank you."

"I'm sorry," the boy said as he looked, bewildered, around the room.

"I know you are. It couldn't be helped. Why don't you wait out on the porch?"

Carter put his arm around the boy's shoulders and took him through the door.

"We'll ride back together, okay?" he said.

The boy looked up and smiled.

"Okay," he said.

Carter returned to the room, and a policeman pointed the way to a bedroom at the back of the house.

In there the chief was squatting next to a man on the floor whose bloody head was propped up on a pillow. An accordian shredded by gunfire lay spread on the bed. An AK-47 was by the big man's side. He had the same broad face as his father, Dieter Stroh. The police chief moved the gun out of reach.

"Hello, Otto," Carter said, squatting on the man's other side.

"You know him?" the chief asked.

The injured man was staring at Carter, a slow angry glow spreading across his face. Suddenly he clutched at a bullet wound in his chest, coughed, and his face went ash white.

"I know of him," Carter said. "By the way, you might want to send your men out front. I knocked out two sentries when I came in. They're under trees, tied up. They may still be there."

The chief nodded at the policeman standing patiently in the doorway. The man left to investigate.

"He went by the name of Ludwig Bretton once he joined Die Wetterfrösche," Carter told the chief. "But his real name is Otto Stroh, a university graduate and musician."

"How . . . do . . . you . . . ?" Stroh mumbled, then he closed his eyes.

"Your father," Carter said.

The eyes opened and stared wearily at Carter. The

anger had left, lost in pain and the tiredness of constantly being a fugitive.

"Was your wife Lina in the living room?" Carter asked. "A little woman, olive skin?"

"Yes! Is she . . . ?"

Carter nodded.

"Sorry," he said. "Looks like you're the last, unless those two sentries survived."

"Joachim and Franz," Stroh said.

His eyes narrowed with thought. He lifted his head suddenly and spit at Carter's face.

Carter ducked, then smiled.

"Looks like you can't do anything right today," he observed.

"I hate all of you!" Stroh shouted. "Every last bastard son of you!" He fell back, pale. A froth of pink blood bubbled at his lips.

"Not one of our usual tourists," the police chief said, smiling wryly, then he turned to look at Carter. "I've called Skopje. They've identified you. A NATO investigator. They'll be here as soon as they can fly up. I assume West Germany will begin extradition procedures."

"I'll live?" Stroh said weakly, his bloody face bathed in sweat.

"Until you're executed," the chief said. "Anything you want to ask him?" he said deferentially to Carter.

"Thanks," Carter said. "Where are the Bulgarians taking Dr. Henry?"

"How should I know what those animals are up to?" Stroh said bitterly. "They're corrupt. You can't trust them for anything!"

"This may be a case of the pot calling the kettle black."

"I don't understand," the chief said.

"Sorry," Carter said. "It doesn't translate well. The Bulgarians hired Die Wetterfrösche to kidnap Dr. Henry. The question is why. Otto?"

Stroh shrugged feebly.

"Don't know. Thought it was a break for us. They paid us a little, and we got to keep her."

"No other payment or incentive?"

"We trade back and forth," the wounded man said.

"Outrageous!" the police chief said, his voice filled with disgust. "How can people act so?"

"Maybe Otto can answer that."

Stroh glared at the police chief and the American agent.

"You're all establishment toadies! You think doing what your governments tell you makes everything okay! Blind fools, that's what you are! You murder freedom!"

"Well, Otto," Carter said, "if this is your idea of freedom, maybe you ought to reevaluate your thinking some. You kidnap and kill. That sounds more like tyranny to me. The worst kind."

Carter stood up.

"You through?" the chief asked him.

"I leave him in good hands," Carter said. "By the way, I think his wife murdered a man in town today. Alex Markov from Skopje. You found him?"

"We got a call, and found the body this afternoon. A friend of yours?"

"Yes."

The chief stood and shook Carter's hand.

"I'm sorry. He was a young man."

"Too young to die."

"Can one of my men give you a lift into town?" the chief continued as they walked to the door.

"Hey, American!" Stroh called suddenly.

Carter and the police chief turned.

"My father," the Wetterfrösche leader said, his voice low with discomfort. "You won't tell him?"

"He's going to find out, Otto. It'll be in all the papers. Your arrest and trial."

The terrorist fell back against the pillow, his face now young and vulnerable. A child who would shame his parents. He frowned, then grimaced. The face went rock hard with determination. He was telling himself he didn't care, but the eyes that stared at the ceiling wondered whether he had ruined himself. He couldn't let the self-doubt last.

"You ought to have a doctor look at your head," the police chief said as he walked down the hall with Carter. He had a sturdy handshake and a sturdy gait. He'd molded his gestures, personality, and stout body to fit his attitude toward life.

"It's better. I'll have it checked after I find Dr. Henry."

"See that you do. You're also too young to die."

In his room at Opatija's Hotel Ambassador, Nick Carter bathed and tended his wounds. He dressed, packed for both himself and Henri Petit, and carried the suitcases down to the lobby where he paid the bill.

The clerk from that afternoon had left early, sick with stomach flu, the new man behind the desk said. More likely he was ill from fear of facing Carter with no information about the dead Henri Petit, Carter reflected as he walked out of the lobby. Cowardice was easier to excuse on a sick stomach.

Carter walked to where he'd parked the Porsche. He hoped that Petit had escaped the Bulgarian sentry his intuition had so accurately knew waited ahead. But more than likely, the Bulgarians had taken him as well as Dr.

Henry with them. In any case, Carter would keep the Frenchman's belongings safe.

She was waiting at the front of his car. Vera Georgiev with the long ebony hair and skin the color of honey, her long legs crossed, a heavy coat covering a skirt gaily decorated with yellow and blue flowers.

"Nikola." She smiled.

"Hello, Vera."

Carter unlocked the trunk and threw in the suitcases.

Vera picked up a cloth duffle bag and tossed it in.

"Sofia?" she asked.

"Looks like it."

"It's a beautiful night for a drive."

Carter locked the trunk and unlocked her door. She slid in gracefully, her legs folding in a flash of skin and petticoat.

"What a fancy automobile," she said as he switched on the motor. She listened appreciatively. "Not like the Russian Lada."

"You've ridden in one?"

"Of course. I lived in Sofia, remember?"

Carter remembered. He drove quietly down the street and out of Opatija through Rijeka and on the highway to Belgrade.

"I didn't kill Alex," she said at last.

"I know. A West German terrorist did. The woman you lost at the nautical store."

"Ah, that one. But why?"

"She was afraid you'd seen her, could identify her. She was just waiting to get you alone so she could kill you, too."

Vera covered her throat with her hand, suddenly silent.

"I'm glad I didn't know," she said.

"And you didn't recognize me."

"No."

"And if you had, you would still have run."

"I didn't know about the missing doctor. NATO. That you worked for NATO."

"The bookstore owner found you later."

"He said you were very suspicious. Asked about Macedonia."

"The store's not a well-disguised front for your organization."

She shrugged.

"It doesn't matter in Opatija," she said. "We have sympathizers there."

"What can you hope to accomplish? There's no way Macedonia will be reunited again. At least not in the foreseeable future. You're spread over three countries."

"No," she corrected. "Three countries have *absorbed* us. Our people are losing their heritage. They think they're nationals of Greece or Yugoslavia or Bulgaria. They've forgotten about Philip of Macedon and his son Alexander the Great, and that we were once united. They're worn down by Bulgaria's failures in the last century. First in the Balkan wars, and then in the two world wars Bulgaria tried to win back all of Macedonia and the territories south to the Aegean. That's where Bulgar shepherds once wintered their flocks, they say. And now Bulgaria's census suddenly shows few Bulgarians in the Pirins being counted as Macedonians. Kalashnikov submachine guns are ready for a new war along the borders there because of it. Only Yugoslavia understands that the Bulgarian government committed statistical genocide on Macedonians. Only the Yugoslavs recognize Macedonians as Macedonians, not Bulgarians, Greeks, or Yugoslavs."

"Your Bulgarian leader Todor Zhivkov claims that Bulgaria no longer has territorial ambitions."

"Ha! You believe him? He claims whatever the Soviets tell him to claim. Right now that suits their political purposes, trying to homogenize Bulgaria. They couldn't do it with Yugoslavia. Why doesn't Bulgaria refuse?"

"A good question," Carter said and smiled. "With committed people like you, it sounds to me like there's a lot right with the country."

She laughed softly and put a long-fingered hand on his leg. The hand was warm, light. She squeezed his thigh.

"I'm glad to see you again, Nikola. Are you glad to see me?"

"Very. Although for a while it looked as if you'd killed Alex."

"My friend," she said simply. "A good man. Decent, you know?"

"I know."

They rode at incredible speeds through the dark and deserted countryside, over mountains rising black to the starry sky. The crescent of the moon slowly made its way across the heavens as the drive lengthened through the night.

"Did you go to Alex because of the jet in the valley?"

She was silent, thoughtful.

"It's a NATO jet," she said at last. "Did you see?"

"Partly. It was covered with brush."

"Still is. Many men come and go. No one seems to know anything. Strangers have come into the valley, and not left. West European strangers, maybe even Americans. I think they were killed. I'm not sure."

"Did your family tell you this?"

"The only thing they talk about is rebuilding. They work from first light to last. It's very hard. Besides, my father has forbidden them to speak about anything that might bring the authorities. He loves me to come home, then he spends the whole time worrying that the police will come to arrest me, and then them, too. In some ways, I've not been a good daughter."

"It's hard to follow your conscience when no one understands."

She shook her head soberly, and fine sleek hairs brushed Carter's cheek.

"I'm so very tired," she said and leaned back in the seat. "I don't remember when I slept last. Maybe I'm rambling?"

"Not rambling. Interesting. When we get to Sofia, we'll find a hotel room and sleep."

She ran her hand up the inside of his thigh.

"Only sleep?"

Carter looked into her dancing black eyes.

"I certainly hope not," he said and grinned.

They drove north around Beograd, called Belgrade by Westerners, and over the Danube through the republic of Serbia in Yugoslavia. The highway angled south toward Sofia, the capital of Bulgaria. The sky was paling into a gray dawn.

Vera dozed fitfully, murmuring in her sleep. Her scent filled the car, an exotic mixture of sun and earth. When she awoke, she stretched like a cat and licked her lips.

"I was dreaming of you," she said and smiled lazily.

"What were we doing?"

"I'll tell you later," she teased. "In Sofia."

Sunrise glowed on the horizon, a bright sunrise of rose and yellow that splattered the land into sparkling green fields and bright blue lakes.

"You haven't told me about Alex and the jet. Did he have information for you?" Carter said.

Vera looked out the window at the rolling countryside, watching a farmer already out with a horse and plow.

"He had information. He gave me a name in Sofia. One of his contacts, a woman there—Lyudmila—but I don't know her. He said he'd tell me more when we met in Opatija. I don't know why he went to Opatija. He went so suddenly."

"To meet me. We worked together, too, sometimes," Carter said. "You can meet your other contact when we get to the city. I'll come with you. She might know something that'll help me find my missing scientist."

"Now Bulgarians have her. I apologize for my country. The men there—I know that's sexist, but the men are the leaders. They have to be good communists to get ahead. They've lived so long being told what to do—pleasing Mother Russia—that they don't stop to think. It's made them stupid, not thinking for themselves. They bungle and make choices they think will please the Russian leaders. Did you know that Bulgaria is so trusted that no Soviet troops are stationed there? The Russians sneeze, and we blow our noses."

"Like the Olympics business."

"Exactly. Less than twenty-four hours after the Russians bow out, the Bulgarians do, too. The first satellite country to follow. We had to show our loyalty first. Ridiculous."

"There's a connection between that jet in the valley and Dr. Henry," Carter said thoughtfully.

"Why do you think so?"

"Because of the mysterious fires on the mountainside. They may have been caused by a laser. And Dr. Henry is a laser expert."

They passed through the Carpathian Mountains, the sky a clear blue, the brilliant sun on their left. Flocks of birds flew overhead. Vegetable and merchandise trucks took over the highway, with small cars fighting to pass the lumbering vehicles.

Suddenly Carter twisted the wheel, and the Porsche sped off onto a narrow side road.

Vera gasped and gripped the dashboard.

"Border ahead," Carter said. "I've got a variety of papers, but none for women. How are yours?"

She bit her lip and stared at him.

"Just as I thought," he said with a smile. "You're used to crossing the border on back mountain trails."

He patted her leg, and they rode the bumpy farm trail at a slow speed for almost an hour. The glamorous Porsche was an unlikely vehicle in the dusty countryside that was populated with farmers behind oxen-pulled plows, flocks of sheep, and women carrying food pails.

Carter saw the brown puffs of dirt clouding the horizon before Vera did. They were in Bulgaria now, and the highway was about fifteen minutes away. But between them and its safety was a small vehicle.

"A motorcycle," he decided at last.

She looked up quickly.

"The militia," she said, her voice low and worried. "What will we do? Perhaps you should let me out . . ."

"It's not just you now," Carter said. "It's the Porsche. It stands out here like an oak in the desert."

They watched the horizon as the brown cloud expanded over the fields and the tiny dot grew into a roaring motorcycle. Carter pulled off the road and stopped. He got out, pressed a valve on a front tire, and the tire hissed air until it was flat.

Vera reached into the trunk and pulled out her small duffle as Carter took out a jack and tire iron. She moved away into a stand of trees. As the motorcycle roared up,

Carter put the jack under the car frame.

The motorcycle stopped. A helmeted militiaman swung his leg over and walked up to Carter.

Carter grinned, pumping the jack.

"Howdy!" he said, then wiped his hands and extended one. "Just like Wyoming. No service stations when you need one," he drawled in English.

"What?" the militiaman said in Bulgarian. He was of medium build with beetling black eyebrows and a scowl on his face. He ignored the hand.

Carter pulled out Balkantourist papers and a passport.

"I'm sorry, sir," Carter said with a deep twang in halting Bulgarian. He handed the papers to the militiaman. "I wanted to see some scenery. Instead I am lost." He waved his hand at the rolling countryside.

The militiaman was reading the fake papers, the scowl deep on his face.

"Is the highway far?" Carter went on as he resumed his pumping.

"Where is the woman?" the man asked, his eyes scanning the trees. He folded the papers into his fist.

"Toilet," Carter said. He spun the wheel and felt for the leak. "My wife has to go to the bathroom a lot." He laughed.

The militiaman didn't.

"Your papers seem to be in order," the man said, watching the trees. "Do you have your wife's?"

Vera waddled out of the trees, her belly big and round from the duffle she'd stuffed under her heavy coat. She held a hand to her forehead.

Carter jumped up, went to her, took her arm. The militiaman watched, the scowl turning to condescending amusement. In all cultures, pregnant women are known for the interesting side effects of their condition. Vera leaned her head on Carter's shoulder.

"How am I doing?" she whispered.

"Pretend you're sick," Carter said quietly.

Suddenly she doubled over, her arms around the duffle that swelled her stomach. She groaned loudly. Carter swept her into his arms, worry lining his face as he carried her to the Porsche.

The young militiaman hurried toward them.

"The car," Carter shouted. "Open the door!"

The man spun around and pulled open the door. His eyebrows were knit with anxiety. Delivering babies wasn't part of his training.

Carter slid Vera onto the seat. Her head rolled back, her eyes closed.

"Got to get that tire changed," he muttered and returned to work.

Quickly, the militiaman and Carter took off the flat and put on the spare from the trunk. As Carter returned the tools to the trunk, the militiaman went to his motorcycle for a canteen. He opened Vera's door and offered her water.

Carter hopped into his seat and turned on the Porsche's motor.

"Thanks, pardner!" he said as Vera sipped again from the canteen.

He saw it just before the militiaman did. Too late, the strap of Vera's duffle bag had fallen below the hem of her coat. The intelligent militiaman looked only a second before he knew what it meant.

Carter reached for Wilhelmina.

The young man ripped open Vera's coat with one hand and yanked his pistol from his side with the other.

For one brief moment that seemed to last an eternity, the American and the Bulgarian stared into one another's eyes.

Each knew the slower of the two was already dead.

Instantly a single shot thundered in the small car. Acrid smoke filled the air as the Bulgarian militiaman flew back from the power of Carter's bullet. The Bulgarian sprawled flat on the roadside, his chest blasted open. Blood poured into the soil as the remains of his shattered heart pumped one last time.

Vera pressed her fist to her mouth.

"Close your door!" Carter said tersely.

She did, and they sped away toward the highway that would take them to Sofia.

TWELVE

While Vera Georgiev phoned her contact to make arrangements, Nick Carter registered at the Hotel Sofia's desk and carried his and Vera's bags down the hall. It was a luxury hotel with the highest standards the Bulgarian capital could offer. Coke machines, a flower stand, a restaurant, and small shops lined the long corridor.

The average annual income in Bulgaria was only a thousand American dollars. Citizens made ends meet through *vruski*, connections. The man who worked in the meat market put aside four steaks for his cousin in the steel plant who could "salvage" an old radio. Each family was permitted to work a small private plot of land to grow vegetables and fruits since much of the nation's produce raised on the big communal farms was exported to improve Bulgaria's hopeless balance of payments.

Carter stopped outside a display window decorated with paper poppies and roses. The Bulgarians' poor economy had inhibited their creation of new products. The hotel's shop window proudly exhibited women's lingerie from Germany, Italy, and France. They were silk garments that would tempt European tourists, not the utilitarian cotton underpants, brassieres, and nightgowns that Bulgarian women were lucky to find in their stores. Tourist money in Bulgaria was courted.

Carter went into the small shop. The woman behind the counter was painting her nails a fiery red.

"I'd like to see some of your merchandise," he said and smiled. "For a tall, beautiful brunette. White and yellow, I think. Bikini underpants. A peignoir set, perhaps. The best you have."

The woman slowly brushed polish across her thumbnail. She shrugged without glancing up.

"Look for yourself," she muttered.

Carter stared down at the top of her head. Bulgarian store clerks, waiters, and hotel staff were state employees. Regular Sofia shops closed on a whim. Customers were an inconvenience when private ownership—and the hope of private ownership—was minimal, and the government paid its poverty-level salaries whether the store made a profit or not.

"I need an expert like yourself," Carter said. "One beautiful woman to help me dress another."

She looked up and smiled tentatively. She had thick features and gratitude in her eyes.

"Well, I'm not sure," she said. "I don't really know what's here."

Together they went through the hanging racks and boxes. Eventually they found a white lace teddy, a yellow bra and bikini set, and a filmy black gown and robe.

"This'll do," Carter said, satisfied.

The woman returned to the counter and rang up the cost. Carter handed her Bulgarian leva.

"Keep the change," he said. "I appreciate your help."

She thanked him with a smile, wistful and bright.

"I hope you come in again," she said. "Anytime."

Carter picked up the bags and packages. He walked to the elevator. Incentive and money were important, he reflected, and together they made business possible and pleasant.

On the hotel's fifth floor, he unlocked the door to the room and went in. Sheer white curtains billowed at the window and swept across the tall double bed with the brass headboard.

He put his suitcase and Vera's cloth duffle on the floor next to it. For a moment he thought of the young Bulgarian militiaman. The young man hadn't reported in, and with luck no one had seen his motorcycle stop beside the Porsche. The death was necessary, but as always troubling.

Carter opened the packages and spread the lingerie on the bed, a lovely display of the elegant life. He went into the old-fashioned bathroom and shaved, showered, and tended his wounds. Vera would arrive soon. Now he allowed himself to remember her hot passion in the Pirin Mountains, the sensual body, the excitement of her demands.

When he returned to the room, he lay naked on the bed, Wilhelmina at his side. The door was locked, the air was warm, and he was exhausted. He closed his eyes and slept, waiting.

A key unlocking the hotel room door awakened Carter. He picked up Wilhelmina, balanced her casually in his hand, and watched the door.

Vera Georgiev walked in, rosy-cheeked, her gay skirt swinging from slender hips.

"Nikola!" Her gaze wavered from his nakedness to the new lingerie and back again.

"Try them on," he suggested, grinning.

"But . . ." She stared at him.

"I insist."

Slowly she dropped her bundles.

She picked up the filmy black nightgown and pressed it against her. She moved gracefully around the room.

"Such loveliness! I've never had anything so beautiful!"

"Here," he said, sliding Wilhelmina under his pillow and rising from the bed.

Naked, he took the gown from her and draped it over the back of an overstuffed chair. He unzipped her skirt and let it fall to the floor. He pulled up her T-shirt, and her glossy hair caught and then cascaded down her shoulders. She looked at him with wide eyes.

He turned her around, unfastened the three hooks at the back of her heavy white brassiere. He slipped the straps down her arms and tossed the bra on the chair. He slid his hands under her cotton panties and over her bottom. She sighed and started to lean back into him. He pulled the panties down her curved legs.

"Step out," he said as if to a child.

She looked at him, puzzled. She lifted one foot, then the other.

"Good," he said and stood up.

"But . . ."

"Raise your arms."

"I don't want . . ."

"Sure you do."

He took her hands and lifted them over her head. Her round breasts swung, pink and full. He dropped the gown over her head.

She was transformed. Her face shone with pleasure. She was a Balkan goddess, tall, haughty, the long folds of her gown draped to the floor. The black of her hair blended with the black of the fine silk until the cloth and woman were one. She stretched her arms and swayed around the room to music only she could hear.

Carter watched, fascinated.

"Come here," he told her at last.

She swayed toward him, her hands extended.

"No," he said.

"Oh?"

"Not yet."

He lifted the gown up her legs, over the downy triangle, over the soft round breasts, and up over her head. He dropped it in a black cloud to the floor.

She stood nude, suddenly shy, before him. A faint blush spread up her neck to the beautiful face.

Carter smiled and picked up the yellow bikini panties.

Meekly she stepped into the scrap of material, and he pulled it up to her hips, arranged it. Tiny curls of black hair decorated the outside of the pale yellow V.

"Lean forward."

She leaned, and he caught her perfect breasts in the lacy cups of the bra.

"Stand up straight."

She stood, and he fastened the single hook.

"Let me see."

She laughed, dancing away from him, spinning and wiggling. A go-go girl. The room was suddenly a disco, and Carter heard in his head the rock music that she danced to, younger than any teen-ager.

"Enough!" he said.

She stared at him, sweat glistening on her forehead and in the deep crevice between her breasts. She ran forward, laughing, and he caught her in his arms.

"Thank you! Thank you!" she breathed against his cheek.

He pulled off the bra and panties while she curled against him. She nipped his earlobe and licked the inside of his ear. He laughed and pushed her away.

"You're not ready yet," he said.

"I am too!"

"Not yet."

She stood back, pouting, and he picked up the white lace teddy from the bed.

"Come here," he said.

Meekly she approached.

He drew the luxurious silk and lace garment up her legs. The cloth was smooth, cool. He arranged her warm breasts, cupped them, lingered. She breathed heavily.

He drew the straps up over her shoulders and stepped back.

The red lips of her mouth parted.

Silently he studied her.

The teddy was cut high on her slender hips. The lace catching her breasts strained, the erect nipples pressing for freedom. Her golden skin gleamed.

She took a deep breath. Desire blazed in her eyes.

"Nikola. I . . ."

Carter picked her up and carried her across the room, tasting her skin, fresh and salty. His heart beat into his ears.

"I can't wait," Vera moaned.

They fell onto the bed. The curtains whipped over them, filled with wind. He rolled her over, her thighs slippery against his.

"I wanted you all last night," she said, hungrily kissing his forehead, eyes, cheeks, neck. "Ever since the mountains," she panted.

He swallowed her lips, the burst of moisture. Unsnapped the crotch of her teddy.

"It's been too long," he said huskily.

She wrapped her legs around him, open and hot, and he entered her as she crowed her glory through the open hotel window to all Sofia.

• • •

The night was bright and cold, twinkling with stars when Nick Carter and Vera Georgiev awoke. He kissed her forehead. She moved like a contented cat in his arms, breathed warm air onto his throat.

"Three times!" she chuckled. "Such a man. And not even an Italian!"

"You've been with an Italian?"

"No. But I've heard."

She lifted the covers and rubbed her hand over his chest, then down between his legs.

"Careful," he said, laughing, "or it'll be four."

She touched and pressed more determinedly. Burning need again spread like hot oil through him.

He yanked her onto him and looked up into the shining black eyes.

"Did you reach the contact?" he said.

"Um-hmm."

Languidly she moved against him, the soft points of her breasts swinging on his skin. Desire filled his head.

"You're a hard woman to keep to business," Carter muttered, breathing deeply.

"Speaking of hard . . ."

He lifted his legs and forced hers apart.

She smiled, her eyes demanding.

"And?" he said.

"And I'm to meet her . . . Oh!"

Her hot wetness enveloped him, swelled him. Her back arched. He rolled her over, rode her, a stallion until once more their triumphant shouts filled the room.

THIRTEEN

Near midnight, Nick Carter and Vera Georgiev walked down a Sofia sidewalk past large buildings with heavily draped windows. The streets were bricked and cobbled. The few pedestrians hustled along in the cold autumn night.

"Over there is the Durzhavna Sigurnost," Vera said, airily waving a hand. "The DS. Bulgaria's security service."

"On General Gurko Street," Carter added with a smile.

She squeezed his arm.

"My lover knows everything!" she said, laughing merrily. "Oh! I feel so wonderful! Even Sofia feels wonderful to me tonight!"

Carter kissed her ear.

"It feels pretty good to me, too."

Their steps echoed on the pavement. Ahead was the Vitosha Hotel and its casino, a gathering place for the secret operatives of the Durzhavna Sigurnost, which was patterned after Russia's KGB. Bulgaria offered the Soviets a wide array of conveniences—secret training camps, arms smuggling through various import-export firms, and even Bulgarian mercenaries for Nicaragua, the Sudan, and other countries of interest to Russia. In some ways Bulgaria wasn't a country in its own right, Carter reflected, despite its obvious national appeals for tourism to boost the nation's economy. Even Balkantourist was rumored to be run by the DS, while officials of the state-owned Balkan Air airline were supposedly working directly for the KGB. As the couple passed the hotel with a half-dozen merrymakers standing on the steps laughing and smoking, Carter threw his arm across Vera's shoulders and pressed her to him protectively. They were just two lovers out for an evening stroll.

At last they came to a small dark house on the outskirts of Sofia. It was unlit, forbidding, with a sense of desertion as if no one had lived there in a very long time.

"Around back," Vera said.

They walked down a driveway smelling of dust. The skeleton of a truck sat in the middle of the drive, rusting in the moonlight, a barricade or a warning.

Carter and Vera squeezed past.

At the back of the building, a small lightbulb glowed dimly above a door. Vera licked her fingertips, shivered, and twisted the bulb off.

The door opened.

"Come in," the deep whiskey voice of a woman whispered. "Quickly!"

Carter and Vera slipped inside. Instantly the door closed.

A short stocky woman turned on an electric lantern, then grinned up at them. A garish slash of red lipstick emphasized the impudence of her smile. She was Lyudmila, the contact Alex Markov had told Vera about.

"Come along!" she announced and, hips swinging, led

them down cellar steps. "You're late!" she complained over her shoulder.

A bar with a single shot glass filled with clear liquid was on one side of the dank room. A phonograph played, and Ella Fitzgerald's voice sang haunting blues. Two round tables with chairs waited beside the record player. The floor's carpet was faded red and threadbare. Three cheap wall sconces lit the room into shadows and pools of light. Money was made there, but not spent there by those who earned it.

"We don't have much time," the woman said. She walked to the bar, tipped the glass, and drained it. "Customers arriving soon."

Across the room, an open door showed a long hallway that ran the length of the building. Doors lined the hall, now closed to the pleasures that lay within. It was a Bulgarian whorehouse. In all countries, there is a black market for sex.

"Want a drink?" the woman said, gesturing at the shelves behind the bar that held various bottles of liquor.

"No, thanks," Vera said. She looked at Carter.

"Another time," he said, "but thanks."

"No other time!" the woman said and laughed raucously. "You won't be back here again. Ever! Understand?"

She'd learned to use good humor to cover the warnings that lay beneath. Danger was part of her business, but she tried to make it palatable for herself and those who joined her in the Sofia cellar. She was a good madam, and a good agent.

"I don't have much for you," the woman said, glancing at the closed hallway doors. "And I'll make it short. It's got something to do with Kintex. They imported supplies to make a jet. A big jet. Paid for by one of our

Bulgarian officials." Her upper lip raised in a sneer. "All very secret. The supplies were only for an exterior and a motor. It could fly, but that's all. No seats. No nothing. Seemed like a big waste, only it's not. They're trying to make it do something special, but I don't know what."

"In the Pirins?" Carter said.

"Yes," the woman said. "They brought a scientist to Sofia. She's supposed to be able to make it stand up and do tricks. But she's not cooperating. So far they're afraid to try much on her. Don't want to kill her and lose her information."

"Dr. Henry?" Vera murmured, looking at Carter.

"Sounds like it," he said. "You're sure about the jet?" he asked the woman.

She laughed.

"Honey," she said, "a man talks two things in bed: nonsense and business. Soon any woman worth her salt can tell the difference, even if he can't!"

"You know a Bulgarian agent— a man that stutters? A deep voice? Baritone?" Carter said.

"Maybe," she said. "Why?"

"He kidnapped the scientist."

"So?"

"Wherever he is, she is, most likely."

"I got it," she said, shaking her head in the Bulgarian affirmative. "Last I heard, he was heading south."

"To the jet?" Vera asked.

"Could be. Don't know for sure."

Vera looked at Carter.

"I need to get to my people," she said. "Make arrangements."

A red lightbulb flashed over the bar. It was the nose on the plaster statue of a Russian bear.

"Damn!" the woman said.

"Customers," Carter said.

"Is there another exit?" Vera asked.

"Are you kidding? This way. Hurry!"

They ran down the hall after Lyudmila. She opened a door and shoved them inside.

"Wait here," she said. "I'll take care of him!"

Lyudmila smoothed her hair, folded her lips over the garish lipstick, and closed the door. Her footsteps pattered away toward the bar.

Vera looked at Carter.

"Alone at last!" she said dramatically.

"For all the good it does us," Carter said and grinned.

They listened at the door and heard the distant sounds of two voices, Lyudmila's and a man's. There was laughter, business being conducted. Then footsteps down the hall. A knock on a door. The door opened. More words, and the door closed softly.

"Come on!" the short stout madam whispered, pulling on Vera's heavy coat sleeve. "Fast!"

They followed her through the bar as Ella Fitzgerald sang of love betrayed, and up the cellar steps behind the electric light. The madam turned out her light and opened the door.

Another man stood there, surprised, a hand raised to the outside lightbulb. An innocent but curious john with money in his pocket and expectation in his face.

"Lyudmila!" he said, staring at Carter and Vera as if he were memorizing them for future blackmail.

Carter swayed, pitching against the doorframe.

"C'mon, honey," he slurred in Bulgarian to Vera.

She giggled and wrapped a hand around his neck.

"Get out of here, you two!" Lyudmila said roughly and shoved them down the step.

"A night on the town, honey," Carter went on, his bulk

hiding Vera as they staggered into the night.

"It'll cost you plenty," Vera said loudly. "But I'm worth it!"

"Get in here, Petkov!" Lyudmila said, then laughed an intimate laugh full of promises.

The door finally closed, and Vera let out a heavy breath.

"Do you suppose he suspects?" Vera asked as they hurried down the driveway and past the abandoned truck.

"A bureaucrat. He suspects everyone," Carter said. "He doesn't even trust himself."

They strode back up the street toward their distant hotel.

"I must get back to Macedonia," Vera said. "That jet could be very bad. Maybe another attempt at Yugoslavia and Greece. Lasers!"

"But it's hollow," Carter said thoughtfully. "Or supposedly hollow. Bulgaria's technology is behind the times. They could be trying to outfit it for a mission."

"If the Soviets are in on it, they'd supply the equipment and know-how."

"They want American expertise," Carter said. "They're gambling on getting the best available. And maybe they're keeping it secret even from the Russians."

They moved rapidly under the distant stars, passing dark buildings, trees heavy with fall foliage, and cars gasping exhaust fumes into the cold night air.

The Hotel Sofia hummed with tourists coming and going. In the restaurant, glasses clinked and people chattered. Bright lights turned the night into day, and the busyness of the establishment allayed the fears of free Europeans in a Soviet-bloc country.

Nick Carter and Vera Georgiev held hands as they rode the elevator toward their fifth-floor room to pack. Passengers talked in German, French, and Italian.

"I'll go to my people," Vera said softly. "That jet must be destroyed."

"Probably," Carter said. "But first I want to check an idea with my superior. More may be at stake here than we realize. I'll drive you south later."

"Can you call from the room?" Vera asked.

"As soon as I get to my suitcase."

"Good. Then I'll go back down and check out," Vera said. "We can leave immediately. There's no time to waste."

He kissed her good-bye as the elevator door opened.

Three other passengers got off with Carter. He strode down the hall and around the corner alone to the room.

He glanced down the stretch of hall and noted that it was empty. He ran his hand along the top of the door and found the spot where he'd left a tiny rolled-up piece of paper. The ball of paper was gone. Either a maid had entered to clean—most unlikely at that hour—or he had visitors. He pulled Wilhelmina from the holster at his back, and his room key from his pocket.

The silence of the hotel's hallway echoed in Carter's ears as he quietly unlocked the door and flattened himself against the wall. He swung the door open.

The room was dark. Quiet.

He slid around the doorjamb and flipped on the lights.

The hand came from behind the door. Sliced through the air. Struck at Wilhelmina. A hand expecting success.

Carter dodged the hand and rammed Wilhelmina into the nose of a dark-faced man with eyes too close together. Blood spurted and cascaded down the disappointed face as the man crumpled uncomplaining to the floor.

"G-get him!" the deep baritone stuttered.

There were four of them altogether. One slammed the

door shut. Another hurtled himself at Carter's legs. They wanted him alive.

Carter crashed his knee into the neck of the one aiming for his legs.

The head snapped back. The neck broke in a loud crack that reverberated in the hotel room. The man collapsed with a thin, piercing scream of pain.

"Q-quit, Killmaster!" the baritone warned as he jammed the cold muzzle of a .45 into Carter's neck.

Carter whirled, knocking the gun from the surprised baritone's hand. He was a tall man, his brutal face scarred with the deep pockmarks of a lost war against acne.

Carter blasted a fist at the stutterer's jaw.

The stutterer ducked. Carter grinned. The man knew how to fight.

The stutterer and the last able-bodied Bulgarian glanced at one another, then converged on Carter from two sides. Hatred and determination blazed from their eyes.

Carter whirled again and kicked the stutterer in the jaw, then blasted a fist into the belly of the last Bulgarian. He heard the satisfying hollow sound of a jawbone solidly hit, and felt the smash of stomach and intestines against the spinal column.

He stepped back.

The four Bulgarians lay sprawled unconscious on the floor. The man with the broken nose groaned.

Quickly, Carter packed his and Vera's suitcases. He could wait for the men to revive so he could question them. But that would also mean waiting for replacements. Someone at the hotel had recognized him and notified the DS. The stutterer wouldn't have known to call him Killmaster otherwise.

Carter needed to get to the jet. That was where Dr. Henry was. If Lyudmila's information about the stutterer's going south were correct, then he had gone and returned. He had returned for one reason: to find a way to make the scientist talk. If the stutterer had returned to transport Dr. Henry from Sofia to the Pirins, he wouldn't be bothering with Carter. He'd have sent underlings. They must be desperate to get the American woman's information.

Carter tied up the three men who would be able to walk when they regained consciousness. The fourth with the broken neck he left to his misery on the floor. Being an agent was no work for the fainthearted, Carter mused.

He closed and locked the door, then went downstairs to find Vera.

The clerk behind the registration desk claimed he hadn't seen Vera Georgiev. He checked his records, looked at Carter's suitcases, and asked whether Carter would like to pay his bill before he left. Carter paid, his eyes moving constantly over the crowded lobby. No sign of Vera. Carter didn't have time to search. He needed to get to Dr. Henry before the Bulgarians decided that torture or drugs and some information was better than no information at all. But Vera! Had she run off? Been captured? Killed?

He stalked to the elevator and punched the button that would take him down to the basement garage. She had friends in Sofia. Macedonian contacts. Here was where she'd grown interested in politics. She could have decided to make a call before checking out. But she would have returned to the lobby by the time Carter came downstairs.

Angrily he marched out of the elevator and over to his forest green Porsche. He kicked the tire. She could need his help right now!

The two thugs got out of an old Lada parked next to the AXE car. Big burly men with blue cheeks in need of shaves. They slammed the Lada's doors.

Carter whirled on them.

"Where is she?" he demanded.

They stopped short, startled by Carter's fury. The stutterer must have left them to guard the Porsche.

"What have you bastards done with her?"

They looked at one another, their brows knitted. They weren't smart, but they were huge, both at least six and a half feet tall. Probably took orders well. And they remembered their orders now. They lowered their heads, took out saps, and slammed them against their palms. They walked menacingly at Carter, slamming the saps, readying them to bash in the American agent's head.

"Can't talk," Carter muttered. "Probably can't read. Definitely can't think!"

The trunk of the Lada suddenly thudded. A dull sound in the quiet garage.

"Vera!"

The trunk thudded again.

"*Mon vieux*!" a faint voice called.

"Henri!" Carter said.

He swung a fist into the first thug's stomach. The man let out a blast of heavily spiced air, then shook his head. He brought the sap down hard on where Carter's head had been a moment before, but Carter was long gone.

Carter kicked the knees of the other thug, then swung and slammed his heel into the first thug's belly. It was hard as a rock.

The two Bulgarians were more confused than hurt.

Carter studied them as they went into a lumbering circle. He backed off, took out Wilhelmina, and aimed down point-blank at the lock on the Lada trunk.

"Watch out, Henri!"

He fired the gun. The Bulgarian thugs rushed Carter.

The Lada's lid popped open. Henri Petit sat up, grinning.

"*Voilà*!" he said. "From Opatija to Sofia. A free trip, and I didn't even solicit it! What good fortune I have."

"Where's Vera?" Carter said as he bent low to crash a fist into the second Bulgarian's groin. The fist hit padding. The Bulgarians were dirty fighters. They expected everyone else to be, too.

Carter raced around the Lada to the Porsche and unlocked the passenger side.

"Get in!" he called to Petit.

"Of course, my Killmaster," Petit said and rose stiffly from the trunk. "I believe some acquaintances of these men escorted your friend Vera into a car and drove off."

As the two Bulgarians chased Carter around the car, Petit picked up the bags and tossed them into the small back seat.

"Great," Carter said irritably. "Unlock my door!"

The two enormous Bulgarians hit upon a plan. They separated and lumbered in opposite directions around the Porsche to head Carter off.

Petit got into the car, slammed his door, and reached across the front seat to unlock Carter's.

"I do think we should leave, *mon vieux*," Petit said as he rolled down his window two inches. "Do you think you could finish them off?"

"I'm trying!"

Carter stood beside his door. The two behemoths charged down on him. They grinned, anticipating success.

Carter waited until the last possible second, then he dodged to the side.

The thugs knew what was going to happen. Shocked dismay lit their faces into near intelligence. It was too late.

They weighed a quarter ton each, and they were caught by their own momentum.

They slammed into one another and bounced apart. Their faces were dazed and angry with disappointment. In a few seconds they'd feel the pain. When a man is that big, everything takes a little longer.

Carter jumped over their twitching bodies and into the car. He locked his door, turned on the ignition, and roared out of the Sofia garage.

FOURTEEN

Nick Carter and Henri Petit drove the AXE Porsche south out of Sofia on Highway 2 under the starry night sky. After six miles they passed Mount Vitosha with its dark forests and continued on into the Rila Mountains on the lightly traveled highway. Automobiles weren't abundant in Bulgaria, and at night they were scarce.

Petit looked out the windows at the passing shadows and infrequent lights. He sighed.

"What a long day it has been," he said.

"But your intuition was right," Carter said, "back at Die Wetterfrösche's safe house. You found your Bulgarian."

Petit chuckled wryly.

"Indeed," he said. "We found each other. I am not as good a fighter as you, Killmaster. I must rely on the intuition instead. When I knew I could not take him, I realized that he wanted me alive. He thought I was you! The amazing Nick Carter!" Petit chuckled again. "I did not enlighten him, and he was very proud of himself for so easily catching the great Killmaster!"

"They want me to help make Dr. Henry talk."

"Exactly! She is becoming notorious. A very tough

little lady. Die Wetterfrösche could not get to her, and the Bulgarians knew that. They hoped to convince you to cooperate with them, and that you'd either trick her or convince her to give them the information they need. I was a poor substitute, but they decided to hold me in case I proved useful to get you."

"That's why they tried to capture me in Sofia."

"But how did they know about us?" Petit said worriedly, tugging on his goatee.

"They didn't know about you. Only me."

The Frenchman looked at Carter.

"There is a leak," he said. "And you know who it is."

"A suspicion," Carter said. "Someone who told them about Alex Markov in Opatija. About me in Opatija, and then in Sofia."

"Ah," Petit said, smiling at Carter. "And who is this unreliable person?"

"I'll let you know when I'm sure," Carter said soberly.

The night moved slowly on the winding mountain highway. Wind whipped the trees. Occasionally Carter passed lumbering Soviet GAZ trucks. In Bulgaria, a two-and-a-half-ton GAZ was often the only vehicle in a village.

Carter saw it before he heard it. A funnel of light chasing down the highway behind them. Then the helicopter's noisy rotors grew in intensity. It was an increasing roar of imminent danger.

"The DS?" Petit said, peering back intently over his shoulder.

Carter pulled the Porsche off under the shelter of heavy pine branches.

"It took them a while," Carter said. "They had to regroup and organize, but they know my car now."

The helicopter swept past, the roar filling their heads

then decreasing as the spotlight rushed down the highway, paused over the few Balkancar and Soviet-made vehicles, then speeded on.

The two agents watched the light disappear around a curve whose mountainside rose in the sharp peaks of trees.

"They'll be back," Petit observed somberly.

"We may be able to outwit them, and if not . . ." Carter shrugged, then opened his door.

"We fight, *mon vieux*?"

"No choice," Carter said, stepping out of the car. "Our job."

Petit nodded and smiled slightly.

"I am relieved to be with an expert."

Carter laughed.

"You do all right yourself," he said. "That intuition of yours has gotten you out of more scrapes than you're willing to admit."

"*Oui*," Petit said with a big grin. "It's true. Thank the Lord!"

Carter walked back toward the center of the pines, pulled out his little radio, and touched the code that put him in contact with David Hawk in Washington, D.C. His conversations with Hawk were secret from everyone.

"N3?" Hawk's voice said gruffly. "Good. You've caught me early. I was just about to leave for the office. Do you have Dr. Henry?"

"Sorry, sir. But I know where she is."

"Tell me about it."

As Carter talked he heard the distant puffing of Hawk on his first-of-the-morning cigar. It was seven o'clock in Washington. Hawk had showered, shaved, breakfasted, and lit the cigar to accompany him on his drive to the office. The head of AXE was always the first to arrive.

"So that damned AWACS jet figures in," Hawk muttered. "I sent an operative into the Pirins. John Bremner. Sent him three days ago. He never reported back."

"Vera Georgiev, the Macedonian agent, said the villagers had seen strangers in the area. They went in. Didn't come back out."

"Doesn't sound promising."

"No, sir."

"An empty jet. No interior. I suppose they could want Dr. Henry to tell them how to outfit it. But they have their own scientists. They're not great, but they have access to Soviet technology."

"Dr. Henry must have something special they're after. She told me in Opatija that she had to get back to her jet in Geilenkirchen."

"That was the AWACS jet Die Wetterfrösche bombed," Hawk said, exhaling noisily far away. "Very special equipment. Had tracking capabilities that would let NATO see far beyond the four-hundred-mile range they've got now. Everything was run by molecular computers—artificial intelligence. Networked laser weapons for defense that could coordinate automatically with the information. It revolutionizes computer informational spying and antiwar technologies. No other country has anything close to it."

"State of the art," Carter said. "I'd say those burning spots on the mountainside were laser burns."

"Ah-hah! Then maybe they *are* outfitting it!"

"They couldn't steal the plans, so they ended up stealing the scientist," Carter said thoughtfully. "Maybe they deliberately exploded that jet, then expected Die Wetterfrösche would have to kill her because West Germany wouldn't meet the terrorists' demands. The threat of a working jet would be gone. The scientist would be gone. And the Bulgarians could speed the building of their own special AWACS-type jet if they could steal the technology from us. They'd be ahead. Then they changed their minds. Something happened to make them believe they needed Dr. Henry for themselves."

"And now they have her," Hawk growled. "You know where she is. Get her back. Intact. We have her work. We're already building a new AWACS. But we don't want to lose her or her future contributions!"

"I understand, sir."

"Nick, you know my situation. I can't send American troops into Bulgarian territory to help you. An international incident and all that."

"I know."

"You'll have to go it alone. Get help wherever you can. Henri Petit is reliable. I've been in touch with his superiors. An unassuming but skilled agent. I don't know much about Vera Georgiev, but we had good reports from Markov on her."

"Yes, sir."

"Keep in touch, N3. I'll do what I can."

The crescent moon was high as Carter returned to the driver's seat of the Porsche. He turned on the motor and they continued their drive south.

"You were gone a long time," Petit observed. "Perhaps reporting in?" He smiled knowingly.

"Right," Carter said. "There was no rush to get Hawk out of bed."

"And what did you and the eminent AXE leader decide?" Petit watched Carter, his gray eyes worried at Carter's quietness.

"It's the same situation," Carter said. "Find the scientist. But now I've got a jet out there I need to look at before I destroy it. Get photos of the interior. It's important to know what technology they've developed."

"I see. Yes. Two assignments make the work more difficult."

"Only more difficult to be successful." Carter smiled at Petit. "And I like to be successful."

Petit nodded. He understood. Success was important to all good agents.

They sped quietly on through the night. Gray clouds formed in thin strips overhead, the stars twinkling as the wind-pressed clouds moved toward the Pirins with the Porsche.

The two agents were relaxed in their seats by the time they passed Rilski Manastir, the Rila monastery that had once been a center of resistance against the Ottomans who ruled Bulgaria for five hundred years. The Ottomans hadn't been popular. They conscripted Bulgarian boys into the Janissaries—elite corps for the sultan—and women into the harem. In 1876 a major Bulgarian uprising finally erupted, but the Ottoman's *bashi-bazouks* massacred the Bulgarians until they were crushed into pacification. It had been the excuse the Russians were waiting for. They liberated Bulgaria in 1878, sacrificing thousands of lives. It was worth it to the czar. Russia pushed the unpredictable Turks farther away from the Motherland and secured the loyalty of the Bulgarians and their descendants. Debt is important to any people, Carter reflected, but eventually honor must become more important.

The spotlight was ahead of them now, rushing back up the highway toward the Porsche. Carter felt Petit stiffen beside him.

"They have returned," the Frenchman said softly.

This time the spotlight moved from side to side along the narrow road, sweeping the area for the Porsche. There were no sheltering trees. the land was barren. A sharp cliff rose to the highway's right. Another sharp cliff dropped off into a black void on the left.

Carter pressed the accelerator to the floor.

"Hold on," he said.

He touched a button on the dashboard that glowed emerald green. The men pitched back against their seats as the G-force of turbojets vaulted the Porsche forward, whizzing the car in a flash through the spotlight and past the roaring rotors of the DS helicopter overhead.

"So fast, *mon vieux*! Perhaps too fast for them to see us!"

The Porsche raced around a gentle curve, tires squealing. Through his rearview mirror, Carter saw the helicopter pause, its spotlight check the highway where the AXE car had been.

His foot to the floor, Carter pushed the Porsche ahead on the winding mountain road, past the blur of rocks, boulders, and scrub bushes. They passed a few cars, local and tourist, angry drivers honking and making obscene gestures to them out their windows.

"What is our destination?" Petit asked, turning to admire a tired female driver whose pretty face had glowed with anger as the Porsche had dashed past.

"A village. About an hour away now. Not far off the highway. Then we hike back up into the mountains where I found the jet."

"Then I will relax," Petit said. "The Bulgarians will remain confused for a while. Such a great automobile! Such a great driver!"

Carter smiled.

"Such an optimistic companion," he said.

A deer stood silhouetted on a crag in the light of the new moon. He shook his antlers and lifted his nose as if to sniff the stars.

"Beautiful country," Petit observed. "Primitive. Untouched. No wonder it attracts tourists looking for out-of-the-way places to brag to their friends about."

The road dipped and flattened into a valley. Tall poplars and pines rimmed a lake the color of indigo ink. A few whitewashed huts glimmered like bleached bones in the distance.

Headlights were ahead, two bright lights speeding forward. Carter watched them. They wobbled, the space between them varying slightly. Motorcycles. One swerved into the Porsche's lane.

"*Mon vieux*, what have we here?"

"Trouble," Carter said tersely.

In his rearview mirror he again saw the spotlight of the DS helicopter. The Porsche raced up an incline. Ahead, behind the motorcycles, was a car speeding as fast as the two cycles.

"May I?" Petit asked, his finger poised on the dashboard's button.

"Please."

The five-inch-wide rectangle appeared on the Porsche's dashboard, glowing inside the dark car. The attack car was ready.

FIFTEEN

From the motorcycles ahead, lethal gunfire streaked red and gold through the night. The bullets whizzed past the Porsche and struck the car's bulletproof exterior with dull thuds.

"What should I do?" Henri Petit asked as he eyed the computer choices on the dash.

"Wait," Nick Carter said.

"A direction I understand." Petit sat back and crossed his arms.

Behind them the helicopter was gaining. Gunfire burst from the big machine. Now there was an erratic hail of bullets from both the front and back. Bullets whined against the Porsche and bounced off.

The helicopter's spotlight found the Porsche at last and centered on it as it continued to close the distance.

" 'Port' and 'Starboard,' " Carter directed Petit. " 'Shield.' "

The Frenchman pressed the silver squares next to the computer commands. The Porsche's controls shuddered slightly as wind resistance met the rising fenders and extending submachine guns over the wheels. Four cross hairs appeared on the dash.

Ahead the motorcycles closed in, aimed head-on at the Porsche. It was a Bulgarian game of chicken.

"*Mon Dieu!*" Petit said softly, then crossed himself.

"Watch the cross hairs," Carter instructed. "Press 'Fire' when you've got something in them."

"James Bond," Petit muttered, fastening his gaze on the dash. "It is better that I do not see what is going to happen anyway."

The motorcycles raced toward the Porsche, close together. The drivers had stopped firing and were bent low over their machines. The tops of their white helmets glowed in the moonlight. They were going to scare the Porsche off the road and into the deep valley lake on one side or into a gas-tank explosion on the other.

In chicken, the driver who wavers first is lost. One moment of indecision is the clue that the opponent waits for. If he sees the other hesitate only once, he knows his nerve is better. He won't quit because he's sure he can triumph.

Carter held the Porsche steady. He knew his car, knew its strength and capabilities.

The motorcycles were fifty yards ahead on the narrow highway.

Then forty.

The one on the right veered, then returned to his course.

Thirty.

Carter held to the center of the highway, trusting the Porsche.

Twenty.

Petit looked up.

"*Mon Dieu*!" Quickly he looked down again to the dash.

Ten.

The motorcycle on the left resolutely kept its path.

Carter gripped the steering wheel.

The motorcycle on the right veered again, whizzing past the Porsche. It was ridden by one of the behemoths from the parking garage of the Hotel Sofia.

The Porsche's submachine guns rattled.

The motorcycle on the left crashed into the front shield of the Porsche, sailing up through the air and over the remarkable AXE car. It was the other behemoth. The car shuddered from the impact and raced on.

Behind the Porsche two fireballs burst into red and orange on the highway. The motorcycles would burn to cinders, the drivers dead.

Ahead the DS car still came at them. The helicopter again opened fire on the Porsche.

Carter pressed his foot to the floor. The valley was ending. The road ahead again curved up into the mountains.

Suddenly the DS car skidded, turned sideways on the road, and blocked it. The helicopter passed over the Porsche, hovering over the stopped DS car. Four men tumbled out of the car and ran to the sides carrying submachine guns.

"Is there enough room?" Petit wondered.

"Don't know."

"Not much shoulder on either side."

The Porsche hurtled forward and streaked through the now silent night.

The four Bulgarians squatted alongside the road, guns aimed.

"Our tires?" Petit asked.

"Probably."

Across the valley another helicopter appeared, its spotlight joining the first helicopter's in a bath of light on the Porsche.

"The odds are terrible," the Frenchman said.

"There's not much you can do to protect tires," Carter agreed, slowing the Porsche. "And I wouldn't want one of those choppers to land on us."

The men looked around the deserted valley for anyone else who could be hurt. They had no choice. To complete their mission, they needed to get past the Bulgarians. That meant eliminating them.

" 'Escape'?"

" 'Escape,' " Carter said.

The French agent hit the button. New lights sparkled on the dash. Readings appeared noting the degree of the road's incline, vegetation, air temperature, wind velocity, and heat transmitted from objects in the surrounding area. Instantly more readings showed . . . HELICOPTER1 [TWO PASSENGERS] . . . HELICOPTER2 [ONE PASSENGER] . . . AUTOMOBILE [EMPTY] . . . TWO MEN EAST [AK-47s] . . . TWO MEN WEST [AK-47s] . . . CONFIRM?

Petit confidently pressed the flashing square.

DESTROY?

Petit looked at Carter, who nodded solemnly. The Frenchman pressed the square.

SUGGESTED LAND SPEED 97 MPH.

"Will it work?" he asked.

"It'll be interesting to find out," Carter said tightly.

Carter again accelerated and steadied out at ninety-seven miles an hour.

The valley flashed past. The Bulgarians kneeling beside the road aimed and fired.

Bullets whined and twanged as the Porsche in the helicopters' globe of light suddenly swerved.

The Bulgarian car blocked the middle of the road. The indigo lake lapped at one side. On the other the road dropped quickly down into flat pastureland. Carter aimed the car there.

Two of the Bulgarians scuttled out of the way.

Computerized gunfire burst from the Porsche.

The two other Bulgarians arced back up into the air, their bodies flying missiles riddled with the Porsche's submachine gun bullets.

The two Bulgarians who ran were caught like fish on spears of revolving bullets. The gunfire blasted them over the lip of the highway and down into the pasture.

Immediately the helicopters resumed firing.

One hovered back on the far side of the Bulgarian car. Like an elegant overweight bird it dropped slowly to block the Porsche from passing the Bulgarian car.

Carter swerved around the car, going straight down the center between the landing props of the descending helicopter. The helicopter's skids scraped the Porsche, resonating like fingers screeching on a blackboard.

"What driving!" Petit exclaimed.

The Porsche's computer sent a backward blast of bullets into the gas tank of the Bulgarian car. It exploded in a ball of flame that lit the valley and showed distant trees stark and skeletal.

Free, the Porsche sped on toward the mountains at the end of the valley.

Henri Petit looked at Carter. Beads of sweat showed on his brow. He smiled with relief.

"We're not out of here yet," Carter cautioned.

The sounds of rotating helicopter blades pursued them.

FINISHED? the computer inquired politely.

Petit pressed the silver square labeled No.

"Correct, *mon vieux?*"

"Correct," Carter said grimly.

One helicopter hovered alongside and above the speeding Porsche. The other took up a position directly above. The computer announced both locations on its screen as the helicopters' guns hurled bullets.

"Your beautiful car will look like it has lost a war with a hailstorm," the Frenchman observed with some of his old aplomb. "Will they never run out of bullets?"

"It'll be a while. They're obviously carrying ammunition."

"I was afraid of that."

Suddenly Carter lifted his foot off the accelerator.

"What are you doing?" the French agent asked.

"An idea," Carter said simply.

He pressed the brake on the car.

NEW INSTRUCTIONS?

Carter touched the Wait square and stopped the Porsche on the highway.

"You are making me very nervous," Petit said, watching out the window as the helicopters landed, one in front of the Porsche and the other behind.

"Our problem," Carter explained, "is that the Porsche doesn't have the capacity to shoot anything in the air. And it doesn't have the speed to outrun helicopters. We're going to make its job simpler."

"Maybe next time it should be outfitted better?"

"Right."

The three Bulgarians bent and ran out from beneath the whirling blades toward the Porsche, AK-47s raised.

Carter rolled down his window.

"Let us pass!" he shouted.

It was a hopeless gesture. Quickly he rolled the window back up as the men raised their guns and fired.

Bullets bounced off the glass.

Carter touched the Escape square again. The computer clicked and hummed a moment in anticipation.

With the Porsche stationary, Carter and Petit could feel the computerized guns move. The blasts gently rocked the heavy car.

The submachine gunfire ripped into the bodies of the Bulgarian DS agents. One of the men was decapitated. Bloody flesh littered the highway. It was over in five seconds.

Carter sighed and drove the Porsche forward around the helicopter. The blades still whipped, ready for takeoff. Again the Porsche's guns moved, shooting into the two crafts' gas tanks. Behind them the helicopters exploded, and again Carter drove the Porsche up into the mountains, leaving behind five blazing balls of fire to light the deserted valley.

Bulgarian cities and villages have a tradition of town squares. The squares are often surrounded by government buildings, one or two restuarants and bars, a statue honoring local or Russian heroes, maybe a Bulgarian Orthodox church, and sometimes a hotel.

The town square of the quiet village that Carter and Petit drove into had only the square and a large rambling house of wood and brick owned by the mayor. They drove past the square and through the village to the outskirts where they left the battered Porsche in the ruins of a farmhouse nestled in a narrow canyon. There were many abandoned farmhouses surrounding the village. In the last twenty-five years, the area's population had dropped from a thousand to two hundred, the victim of poverty-ridden people moving to cities in search of work, and of a low birthrate that frightened the Bulgarian national government into offering monthly stipends to couples who bore children.

The two agents piled brush over the Porsche, changed

their clothes, put supplies and belongings into backpacks, and set out on a rough trail up the canyon. Carter led the way over the familiar terrain.

"It is so quiet here," Petit observed. "Peaceful."

"A relief," Carter agreed, knowing Petit, too, was remembering their close call in the valley an hour earlier.

"Such stupid men, those Bulgarians. Too often, stupidity leads to death."

"And they weren't trying to take me alive," Carter said.

"Do you suppose that means that Dr. Henry has told them what they want?"

"I hope not," Carter said, striding up the trail faintly visible in the moon's light.

Two and a half hours and ten miles later, the two agents came to the clearing where the Georgiev farmhouse had been. They went into the manger and fell on the straw, exhausted. The cold mountain wind whipped through the manger. Insects and birds chirruped and sang. In the distance, cattle lowed. Carter thought about Vera, about their time here and in Sofia.

"Another long day, my friend," Petit said with a sigh as he burrowed into the straw.

"At daybreak we find the jet," Carter said. "Make plans."

The Frenchman nodded and closed his eyes. The two agents slept.

SIXTEEN

A pink haze slowly rose on the gray dawn horizon as Nick Carter and Henri Petit squatted on the ground hidden by brush, binoculars to their eyes. They studied the long valley that contained the AWACS jet.

Bulgarians in uniforms, coveralls, and dark DS suits worked around the jet and a squat prefabricated headquarters building painted in brown and green camouflage colors. Six Bulgarians walked a regular patrol around the jet. Others sat on boulders or leaned against trees keeping watch from the two mountainsides rimming the valley. Three jeeps and a big GAZ truck were parked near the headquarters. Small tents were staked behind the building. A dirt road without the ruts made by years of travel trailed down the center of the valley. About a mile off it dropped out of sight.

"How do they expect to get the jet out of here?" Petit wondered. He moved his binoculars down the valley.

"There," Carter said. "See how the trees are turning brown? They've been cut at the trunks, then propped up as if they were still alive."

"They should have sprayed the leaves green," Petit observed.

"The Bulgarians can push the trees away easily using that bulldozer. They've already moved rocks and boulders. They can fly out of here anytime."

Petit nodded solemnly.

Two women came out of the headquarters. It was Vera Georgiev and Lyudmila, the agent from Sofia. Their hands were tied behind their backs. Two DS men walked on either side of them toward metal-sided latrines directly below Carter and Petit. The women stared straight ahead.

"That answers one question," Carter said.

"Your Vera? I do not think they have hurt her."

"Thank God. The other woman runs a whorehouse in Sofia. She was Vera's contact."

"Vera was traced through the madam?"

"Probably."

Petit sat back on his haunches and looked at Carter.

"Well, *mon vieux*, how shall we proceed?"

The two agents talked quietly, occasionally glancing down at the Pirin Mountain valley, as Carter gestured and explained his plans.

"All that in the full light of day?" the Frenchman asked. He looked at the guards on the mountainside.

Carter clapped him on the back and handed him the roll of striated tape.

"Use that intuition of yours," he said and smiled.

Slowly Nick Carter made his way down the rocky mountainside. His gaze moved up from his treacherous footing to check whether he was noticed and then back again to his feet. He moved stealthily from one protective boulder to another, keeping trees for a shield whenever possible. About thirty yards away, Henri Petit also circled carefully down toward the valley.

The aroma from the latrine moved with the wind, a

heavy smell of untreated human waste. The women entered the prefabricated building, their guards waiting outside. The two DS men lit cigarettes and laughed.

Carter padded to a stop behind the structure. Inside, the women were talking in subdued voices. Carter tapped on the wall. The women were silent.

"Vera. It's Nicola."

Again the women talked, an argument in soft but strident tones. At last Vera's voice predominated.

"Where've you been?" Her whisper was teasing but full of worry.

"Stay inside," he told her. "Keep back from the wall. We're going to get you out."

"There are two of us," she said.

"I know. Be patient."

A dog barked. Not far away, Henri Petit moved from tree to tree, closing in on the back of the latrine. Carter nodded to him as the Frenchman took out the roll of tape.

Carter walked around to the side of the latrine to keep watch. The Bulgarian guards were still laughing and talking in guttural voices about the women.

The dog barked louder. Petit turned in the direction of the sound, then hurriedly applied strips of tape in a big rectangle on the latrine's metal wall. Carter took out his little gas bomb, Pierre, then reached into the side pocket of his backpack.

Rope flying from his neck, the ends frayed from chewing, the Doberman pinscher tore through the trees toward Carter.

The two DS guards turned, alert, their rifles ready. Other men in the compound looked around to see what the commotion was.

A man stepped out of the door of the headquarters. Carter didn't have to look long to know who it was.

Atanas Gelassi, supposedly the number-four man in the Bulgarian national government and the favorite of Chairman Todor Zhivkov, the country's leader and First Secretary of the Bulgarian Communist Party for more than thirty years.

The DS guards stalked around the latrine.

Carter backed up.

The sharp smell of ozone suddenly filled the air. There was a dull thud. The special AXE tape had melted the metal, and the rectangle had fallen to the ground. Petit would lead the women up the mountainside, but he needed time for stealth. The commotion had to end, the valley had to quickly return to normal.

Carter opened the can of C-rations from his backpack and waited for the dog and the DS guards.

They appeared simultaneously before him. The dog's fur stood straight up, his lips drawn back in a snarl over glistening fangs. The guards aimed their rifles at Carter's heart.

"Halt!"

"Who are you?"

"Wizard!" Carter said, then tossed the C-rations at the dog's feet.

Carter backed up again. The dog sniffed the food and cocked its head. The Bulgarians pursued Carter one calculated step at a time to the hidden back of the latrine.

Pierre behind him, Carter pulled the pin and dropped the gas bomb while the Bulgarians glared menacingly at him, the inadequate person's attempt at intimidation. The bomb would go off in thirty seconds.

"It's a long story," Carter told the men in Bulgarian, smiling as they stared astonished at the gaping hole in the latrine's wall.

They were obviously not the brightest the DS had to

offer, assigned to guard women—the second-highest life form. But their rifles evened the odds their intellects had handicapped them with.

Carter kicked the rifle from the nearest, then spun and lashed the rifle from the second. He heard Pierre's ominous click as the men recovered and swung their fists.

With two neat chops, Carter knocked the men to the ground and into Pierre's cloud of gas. One breath each, and the men gagged and fell.

Carter strode to the side of the latrine again.

"Wizard," he called. "Come."

Tail wagging, the former wonder dog lowered his head and meekly approached Carter. Out of sight of the compound, Carter scratched the dog's ears and listened. Sounds of work and shouted orders showed that the Bulgarians in the valley had lost interest in the noisy dog. The lack of gunfire had indicated to them that all was well with the DS men guarding the women. Wizard looked at Carter and cocked his head, puzzled. No one had attempted to retrain him as an attack dog yet. Probably they wouldn't bother. Once the jet was gone, he would be left behind to find another home.

Carter opened another can of C-rations, picked up the empty can from the ground, and walked back around the latrine. He dumped the new food on the metal rectangle for the dog, stuffed the cans that would identify him as American in his backpack, picked up the exhausted Pierre for the same reason, and climbed the mountainside.

Carter met Petit, Vera, and Lyudmila at Vera's family's farm. Vera threw herself into Carter's arms, and he held her to him.

"They told me they had you, too!" she cried.

He stroked her long black hair.

"Not yet," he said. "We need to leave here and find a hideout. They'll come looking for you. Can you contact your Macedonian irregulars?"

"If I have a radio," she said, black eyes narrowing in thought. "You have a plan?"

"It'd better be a good plan," Lyudmila observed. Her bright red lipstick was gone, her hair disheveled, her dress wrinkled from sleep. "Maybe I can help if I know what it is."

"First I need information," Carter said. "I want to talk to your father, Vera."

She lifted her eyes in mock horror.

"You *are* a brave man," she said and smiled.

Swiftly she led the way past the laser-burned circles, fallow tobacco fields, and slopes with grayed tree stumps. Birds fluttered and sang. A flock of goats tended by a shepherd grazed nearby. At last the group of travelers came to a whitewashed cottage with strings of red peppers hanging in the windows.

Near the cottage a woman with a brown shawl over her head gathered twigs into her arms. Across the farmyard Vera's father squatted in the dirt, stirring a cauldron of hot tar and pine oil. His large weathered hands were raw with the tiny cuts that come from cold weather, hard outdoor work, and no gloves.

He glanced up at the small group as they circled around him. His face was expressionless. He resumed his stirring.

"For the sheep and goats," he said, nodding at the pot. "Good medicine to treat their injuries."

"I want to know about the jet," Carter said.

"It is a good life here," the farmer went on. "We like it this way. No trouble." He looked directly at Vera. "You shouldn't have come this time."

She bit her lip, her face stricken. Lyudmila put an arm around her shoulders.

"You're frightened," Carter told the man. "Having the jet here has destroyed your people's peace."

The farmer stared at Carter, worry etched in his weathered face.

"You saved Maritsa, and I owe you. I'll answer your questions, then you must go. And never return."

"I understand," Carter said. "When did the jet leave the valley?"

"You know, then," the man said. "It flew out five days ago. Dusk."

"And returned that same night?" Carter asked.

"It shook the mountainside, disturbed the animals and women."

Carter looked at Vera.

"You have a good daughter," he told the Bulgarian farmer. "Every man should be so lucky. When this is over, she will be able to visit you safely."

Carter wheeled away, and Vera, Petit, and Lyudmila followed him back to the trail and around a bend. Vera took over there, and they scrambled off the trail and over rocks as she led them to a hidden place only a child who'd grown up exploring the mountains would know. They stopped in a clearing sheltered by boulders where they could look down over another valley where a sparkling stream ran into a pond.

"Come with me, Vera," Carter said. "We'll be right back," he told Petit and Lyudmila.

"Shouldn't we stay together?" Lyudmila asked, worry in her voice.

"You will be safe with me," Petit said and grinned. He looked at Carter knowingly, then nodded. His intuition had accurately assessed what Carter had figured out. "I am a gentleman!"

Vera slipped her hand into Carter's, and they walked a short distance out of sight.

"I'll talk to my people and order the necessary equipment," he said as he got out the radio. "Then I want you to contact your Macedonians. Here's what I want you to tell them."

Near the bottom of the road that led up into the valley where the AWACS jet was hidden, Carter handed Wilhelmina to Lyudmila. They were alone; Vera and Petit were back on the mountainside waiting to fulfill the assignments Carter had given them.

"You understand what you're to do?" he asked.

She nodded somberly, then her eyes crinkled with anticipation.

"A heroine, eh?" She laughed.

"That's it."

They walked up the road, Carter's hands raised high, Lyudmila pointing the Luger at his back. She held the gun comfortably, familiarly, as if she were nostalgic for her own. Workmen ahead stopped to stare. Some ran back toward the headquarters.

"I always wanted to be a heroine," Lyudmila said, her voice gay. She walked with soft plopping steps, her stout legs rolling with the land. "It's crazy I ended up in the business I did."

"But you like it."

"Bulgaria is a good country. A country that admires heroes. There aren't many heroines."

"A tragedy of prejudice," Carter observed.

"Perhaps. But someday I'll be recognized. A woman.

There are many of us.'' She squeezed Carter's buttock. ''And we don't have to leave our marks only in bed!''

Carter turned and chucked the sturdy Lyudmila under her double chin.

''If you give it up,'' he said with a hearty laugh, ''I'm sure your mark will be missed.''

SEVENTEEN

Atanas Gelassi was a man of medium height and thick wrists. His dark hair receded above a Slavic, aristocratic face magnificent with purpose. The eyes were icy, analytical. He smoked a Stewardess cigarette, leisurely blowing rings into the morning air as if he owned not only the compound but the world. He stood outside the headquarters building, waiting for the group. He showed no impatience. He was a man who was comfortable with his power.

Behind him the stutterer lounged against the doorjamb, his pocked face as immobile as stone. But his eyes blazed hatred at Nick Carter as he cradled his AK-47 and slowly swung it around. He lifted it, aimed it at Carter, gave a short barking laugh, and lowered it again, pleased with his joke.

Nick Carter and Lyudmila were surrounded by an escort of silent DS men who carried their guns as casually as if they were still farmers carrying their hoes. The group made its way toward Gelassi.

"Nick Carter," Gelassi said, allowing his mouth to smile. He looked at Lyudmila as the group stopped in front of him. "You've come back to the nest," he told her.

"The bird of prey," Carter said. "A double agent."

"You knew?" Lyudmila said, her round fat face astonished.

"It had to be you," Carter said. "Only you could have tipped off Die Wetterfrösche that Alex Markov had gone to Opatija to meet me. You knew where he'd be staying. And you knew because he'd just been in touch with you to get information for Vera. It took them longer to find out where I was staying in Opatija. I wasn't there, so they kidnapped Petit."

Lyudmila's eyes narrowed. The stutterer watched with interest.

"And you joined Vera after she was caught in Sofia," Carter went on, "and acted as if the DS had caught you, too, so you could pump her about me. That's why the argument in the latrine. You couldn't figure out how you were going to alert your friends here without blowing your cover. Then you decided to go along and wait for the opportunity to get all of us."

"You take big chances, Killmaster," Gelassi observed, blowing a smoke ring. "But this time you have no chance. You are already dead."

"Allow m-me, sir," the stutterer said eagerly, and he stepped forward, the AK-47 tight in his hands.

"Not yet," Gelassi said curtly. He looked at Lyudmila who was trying to figure an advantage to the situation. "How many of them are out there now?" he asked her.

"Two," she replied. "Vera Georgiev and Henri Petit. They're back on the mountain. They've got some kind of plan worked out. I think she's called in the Yugoslav Macedonian fighters."

"And you don't know what the plan is." Gelassi scowled as he realized she'd come without important information.

Lyudmila had no advantage. She was in trouble. Her cheeks trembled.

"He . . . Carter planned everything out of earshot! He fixed it so I couldn't hear," she said. Her eyes moved around Gelassi, never focusing on him. "But I caught him! I brought him here!"

The stutterer barked another laugh.

"I'll get the information f-for you," he told Gelassi, stroking the AK-47.

"Just like you get information from Dr. Henry?" Carter said mildly. "Die Wetterfrösche already failed at threats and torture. That's the only effectiveness you have."

"You walked into the valley here on your own, Carter," Gelassi decided, no longer interested in the stutterer or in Lyudmila. Her worth had plummeted. She knew it, and her plump face creased with worry. "Is this part of your plan?" Gelassi asked Carter.

"Of course," Carter said. "Shall we talk?"

Atanas Gelassi's office had one window behind a metal desk piled with papers. Gelassi sat in his chair and crossed his legs. He motioned to the guards who had followed them into the room.

"Metodi stays," he said. "The rest of you find Petit and Georgiev. Ask Lyudmila. She can't be completely stupid."

Gelassi swiveled in his chair as the guards left. He looked out the window at the rough mountainside as Metodi, the baritone stutterer, took up a post at the single door.

"All right, Carter," Gelassi said. "What are you offering?"

"A story," Carter said. He pulled up a folding chair

and sat. "It's about ambition and cleverness, two qualities unique in a country of servants. And about a brilliant sting operation that almost worked."

Gelassi turned and gazed speculatively at Carter. He took a cigarette from his pocket and held it in front of his lips. Metodi came from the door and pulled up a lighter from inside his jacket. It was strung conveniently on a chain around his neck like an ornament. In Bulgaria, smoking was one of the few vices that was easily supplied. The nation grew so much tobacco that it was the world's leading exporter of cigarettes. Metodi snapped the lighter, watched his boss inhale, closed the lighter, and returned to the door.

Gelassi's gaze never wavered from Carter. He smoked. It was something he did, like eating regularly, reading reports, and killing people. Part of life. He didn't particularly enjoy it.

"Go on," he said without humor.

"You hired Die Wetterfrösche to kidnap Dr. Henry," Carter said, taking out one of his own cigarettes and lighting it. He inhaled, savoring the rich taste of the custom-blended tobacco. "Your people offered to provide the diversion for the kidnapping. A partnership. They kept Dr. Henry. You kept what you wanted. You flew a stripped-down AWACS copy from this valley to Geilenkirchen. If someone were to check the records, I'm sure they'd find an AWACS reporting in at Geilenkirchen in transit to another destination just before the kidnapping. No one there would've thought to follow up on the jet once it left. Too much confusion. Am I correct so far?"

Gelassi blew a smoke ring.

"I'm still listening," he said noncommittally.

Carter smiled. The Bulgarian leader was all intellect and ambition. The ideal type of man to organize and pull off such a complicated, dangerous plan. Carter had found the right person. Now he needed to get more information and stall long enough so that the Macedonians, if not intercepted or caught, could reach the area.

"Good," Carter said. "Die Wetterfrösche exchanged jets. They moved Dr. Henry's special AWACS to where your stripped-down version was parked, then they exploded the fake AWACS."

Gelassi's eyes flickered with surprise at Carter's accuracy.

"Everyone there would've thought it was the real jet," Carter went on. "Your crew flew out with the specially equipped AWACS to their supposed destination. Instead they brought it here. No one suspected the whole point of the sting was stealing the jet. Then the trouble began."

Gelassi was impressed. The Bulgarian rolled the tip of his cigarette in an ashtray and studied Carter thoughtfully.

"You're a bright man, Carter. Not an ordinary thug. You deserve your reputation. Tell me how you figured this out."

"Various things. The burned spots on the mountain when your people were trying to use Dr. Henry's equipment. Your need to have Dr. Henry herself because you hadn't counted on the level of sophistication of the equipment. And then there was the information that a jet left the valley and returned the same night five days ago when Dr. Henry was kidnapped."

"Ah, yes. Sound deduction. And what do you plan to do about it?"

"Nothing now. But soon."

Gelassi stood up and walked around the desk. He stopped in front of Metrodi.

"You see here a good Bulgarian," Gelassi said, turning and looking at Carter. "Loyal. Reliable. Ready to do whatever his country needs."

"Whatever *Russia* needs," Carter corrected.

Again Gelassi smiled.

"You are astute. Yes, whatever Russia needs."

"Your Bulgarian Chairman Zhivkov is old and ill. Either he'll die soon, or he'll be replaced."

"I am not the logical choice," Gelassi said and returned to his chair. "It is unfortunate because I am the best successor. Even Zhivkov wants me. But not now. In a decade. Perhaps longer. After someone older, more experienced, has had a chance."

"A severe disappointment to a man of your capabilities."

"That is one way of expressing it," Gelassi said, smoking. "More logical is that I would simply be better at the job. I have a degree in economics. I was the youngest Party member in my graduating class. I have prepared myself for thirty years. Since I was a boy, I have thought of nothing else but to lead my country. None of the others has my dedication, education, and abilities."

"But they're loyal Communists. They've paid their dues."

"If it would help, I would eliminate them," Gelassi said.

"Kill them, yes. But then the Russians wouldn't like that. You'd be killing the people they'd chosen. Much better for them to live, and for the Russians to recognize your greatness and promote you above them."

"Exactly," Gelassi said. "You must recognize that there is no way you can stop me."

"Perhaps, but you do have some problems," Carter said and smiled. "You can't call in reinforcements because you still don't have the jet working. If you let Sofia know you need help, they'll ask questions. They'll find out about the jet, take the credit, and all your work will be for nothing. And you can't give it to the Russians until you know how to run the equipment. Otherwise, you'd be laughed at—'a good thief, but he can't do anything more.' "

A flush rose up Gelassi's aristocratic face.

"You expect unsophisticated Macedonian farmers to stop my people?" Gelassi said. "Then you are a fool!"

He had a point, but Carter didn't dwell on it.

"What I expect is of little consequence to you if you're so confident in your abilities," Carter said.

It was a challenge. An intellectual challenge. The only kind that interested Gelassi.

Gelassi stubbed out his cigarette.

"What are you offering?" the leader said, his eyes glittering.

"What you want. Dr. Henry's information." Carter leaned forward in his chair. "My orders are to get her alive. We want her future work. I'll talk her into teaching your people how to use the equipment in exchange for our freedom. The Macedonians won't come in if I give the signal."

"Then you would like a fake escape," Gelassi said thoughtfully. "It would make you look good. Your agency would never have to know, and my payment would be to ensure my position after Zhivkov dies."

As he spoke, the corners of his lips curled in what was intended to be a smile of agreement, but Carter knew that the Bulgarian planned to break that agreement once he had what he wanted. There would be no escape. He would kill Carter and Dr. Henry. He would kill Zhivkov if he could get away with it.

"Very well," Gelassi said coolly. "I give you twenty-four hours."

Twenty-four hours was what Carter needed.

"Forty-eight would be better," he said and smiled.

"One day only," Gelassi said. He nodded toward Metodi. "Take him to the jet. He can see it all."

Carter was dismissed. He left, pleased and worried.

The inside of the AWACS jet was quiet, the rows and rows of computer and radar consoles shut down. No sparkling buttons of light. No humming machinery. Just dark, blank screens and keyboards. It was a tomb, a monument to unfathomable technology housed in the enormous hull of a Boeing E-3A.

Carter strode down an aisle toward a bright light that illuminated the front of the aircraft. Metodi followed closely, his pocked face leering evilly. The air smelled of cigarette smoke and machinery.

Dr. N. R. Henry was strapped to a chair, her head fallen forward. IV tubes dripped liquid into both arms. A DS man stood guard next to her. He smoked. Dead cigarette butts littered the floor.

"If I had my way, you'd be d-dead now," Metodi said, jamming the barrel of his AK-47 painfully into Carter's back.

"Did Gelassi tell you he'd make you head of GS when he gets elected?"

"He could d-do worse."

The DS guard watched with interest. The only excitement in a long, boring watch.

"He could do much better," Carter said mildly. "I assume that you were the one who set up the helicopters and motorcycles that tried to take me back on the highway. Not great planning on your part."

Metodi growled and raised a fist.

"Temper," Carter warned him. "Gelassi says you can't touch me."

Metodi looked at the fist, his face enraged with sudden frustration. He dropped it, then smashed the butt of his AK-47 through a wall. Fiberboard splintered and crumbled to the floor.

"I'll get you, Killmaster!"

Carter laughed.

"I can't be bothered," he said. "I have grown-up work to do."

He knelt in front of Dr. Henry. Her dinner pumps were gone, the long skirt tattered. Her face was drawn and bruised, the eyes closed.

"Dr. Henry," he said softly in English. "Can you hear me?"

EIGHTEEN

Deep in her throat, Dr. N. R. Henry gurgled. It was an animal sound, unintelligent, painful with defeat.

Nick Carter cupped her chin and lifted the bruised face.

"Dr. Henry," he said again. "It's Nick Carter. I'm going to free you."

She opened glazed eyes.

"Everything's going to be all right," he said.

"I've . . . told them . . . how—"

"Don't worry about it," Carter said. "You haven't told them enough yet to do much good. Now you've got to hold on for just a little while longer."

"I . . . don't know that . . . I can. The drugs . . ."

Metodi shoved the barrel of his gun into Carter's neck.

"Talk in German or Bulgarian," he ordered roughly.

"Worried?" Carter asked him in his own language. "Your boss isn't. Don't you trust Gelassi?"

Metodi glared at Carter. Slowly he withdrew the AK-47. Carter again looked into Dr. Henry's sad eyes.

"Dr. Henry," he said. "Nancy. Your name is Nancy?"

She nodded feebly. She was a slight woman to begin with, but the ordeal of the last week had made her as light and fragile as an autumn leaf.

"I'm Nick," he went on. "You've done as much as any human can. You should be proud of yourself."

It was important that she have hope again.

"I want to go home," she said dully. "I want to see my family. My work . . . will I ever be able to work again?"

"You'll do both," he told her firmly. "Look at me. Do you believe me?"

She stared into his eyes. Disbelief and hope fought a war on her ravaged face. At last she sighed. She'd made a choice.

"Very well," she said, her voice quavering. "I'll do the best I can."

"Good. That's all any of us can expect."

She nodded and closed her eyes, exhausted. A faint veneer of peace had settled on her small features. It wouldn't last, but it was a respite that would help strengthen her. Slowly her head drooped again and she slept.

Carter stood and looked at Metodi.

"Well, Number Two," he said in Bulgarian, "the first thing you've got to do is pull these tubes out of her arms. As long as she's doped up, she won't give us any information that's sensible. And then I'd like a nap. How are the accommodations around here?"

"Y-you won't be c-cocky long," Metodi threatened as he ordered the guard to remove the IVs. He shoved Carter back down the jet's aisle.

The noon sun hung heavy overhead, its heat distant in the autumn mountains. The sky was a cold sapphire blue. Birds sang and insects chirruped, reminding the world that there were better ways to live than what those in this valley planned.

Somehow, Carter had to provide a diversion in the compound to give the Macedonian fighters a more even chance. He had to rely on his inventiveness. If the diversion were good enough, then Dr. Henry would be rescued and Carter would be able to fly the AWACS out and return it to Geilenkirchen where it belonged.

Carter and Metodi walked back across the compound toward headquarters. Guards patrolled the jet and the valley walls. Workmen carried papers, checked vehicles, and unloaded ammunition. The aroma of cooking lamb and vegetables came from a wide kitchen tent.

Lyudmila was walking across the compound, her shoulders slumped. Her raucousness was gone, replaced with dejection. It was impossible to be a heroine when your triumphs weren't recognized and your opportunities eliminated.

"Lyudmila!" Carter called to her.

Metodi poked the gun barrel into Carter's back.

"K-keep moving," he growled.

Lyudmila hesitated, looked at Metodi, then Carter.

"Remember!" Carter called. "To be recognized you need to do something spectacular!"

She looked at him curiously, her round face pinched in thought. She was mulling over the hint. Her ambition was great enough that Carter hoped she would eventually figure it out.

Carter and Metodi continued past her and into headquarters. The building was divided into three sections. To the right was the closed door of Atanas Gelassi's office. Outside it in an open room were two desks with young GS officers behind them, typing reports. To the left was a hallway.

Metodi prodded Carter down the hall, opened a door at the end, and shoved Carter in. Being physical made Metodi feel intelligent.

"Stew here, Killmaster," Metodi said. "It's the last room you'll ever have!"

Carter laughed, and Metodi's dark eyes shot daggers of hate in reply. The Bulgarian closed the door with a bang, and the lock clicked into place.

Carter stretched out on the single cot and sniffed the air. The sensuous musk that lingered told him that this was where Vera—and Lyudmila—had been kept.

Heavy footsteps came down the hall and stopped outside Carter's door. His guard was in place. Carter lit a cigarette and smoked. His cigarettes were all that Gelassi had left him. The leader had supervised Carter's search. The backpack, Wilhelmina, Pierre, and Hugo were all in Gelassi's office, far away from the ingenuity of the Killmaster.

Carter worked over the problem in his head. Technicians would soon go to the AWACS to retrieve Dr. Henry. She'd be hauled back to headquarters and locked behind a door for safekeeping until Carter was called to talk to her. The drugs would take hours to wear off.

Meanwhile, the Macedonians would be making their way across the border into Bulgaria, using all their mountain knowledge and the years of secrecy that had kept their small bands in existence. Barring mishap or capture, they should be in place around the valley by dawn tomorrow. Vera and Petit would lead them from both mountainsides to attack the Bulgarians and rescue Dr. Henry before the morning session of questioning began.

But the attack could easily turn into a bloodbath and Macedonian rout. The Bulgarians had the advantage of entrenchment. The only Macedonian advantage was surprise. At this point, the odds were not favorable. Carter's purpose in coming to the valley was to at least even the chances.

He got up and stretched at the barred window. Below him Wizard slept in the sun. The sleek Doberman was tethered to a stake at the back of the headquarters building where his barking would be less annoying.

"Wizard," Carter called softly. "Wizard."

The big dog raised his muzzle and looked questioningly at the window. He stood, shook, and walked to the window, his tail wagging. He was on a ten-foot tether.

Carter glanced around the room. He stripped off the pillowcase from the cot's pillow and knotted it into a ball.

"Do you remember how to fetch, Wizard?"

The dog cocked his head and lifted his front paws to the windowsill. He stretched his head in between the bars. Carter scratched the dog's ears and rubbed his muzzle. He showed the animal the pillowcase ball and let him smell it.

Carter threw the ball out the window into the dust.

"Fetch, Wizard!"

The dog leaped down and pounced on the ball. Tail wagging, head high with canine pride, Wizard returned the pillowcase ball to Carter's hands.

"Good boy!" Carter said and again scratched the dog's ears.

The dog panted and wagged his tail happily. There was a scurrying sound of footsteps beyond Carter's view. He craned his head as Wizard licked his hand.

"Bored, Killmaster?" Lyudmila said quietly as she approached the window, gazing nervously over her shoulder.

"Lost, Lyudmila?"

She looked at him, disappointed. She'd come for a reason, and Carter hadn't given her the immediate opening she'd expected.

"They're watching me," she said breathlessly, her eyes constantly moving up and down the back of the building.

"What's in it for me?" he said.

That was a response she could deal with. She grinned.

"I can't let you out," she said. "And I won't bargain until I know what you have in mind."

Carter ran his hand up over Wizard's muzzle to the back of the dog's head. He patted him.

"Okay, boy. Down!"

Wizard blew hot breath in Carter's face, then dropped obediently to the ground. He circled twice, then stretched out to resume his nap in the sun.

"You're done with Gelassi," Carter observed. "You'll get no recognition from him even after the chances you've taken. But you're still a DS agent in good standing with Sofia."

"Correct," she said eagerly. "But they're there, and I'm here. I can't get to a radio. They're too well watched. Besides, I'd only get myself into trouble with Sofia if I called them in at this late date."

"Not necessarily," Carter said. "You've got something valuable to give the men in line to succeed Zhivkov. You can use my radio. It's in the backpack in Gelassi's office. Then here's what we'll do."

The afternoon passed slowly. Nick Carter's small room filled with the heat that collected under the headquarter's aluminum roof. He thought of Dr. Henry, imprisoned in the jet, and worried about her. Occasionally Wizard stuck his head through the bars, bored, asking for attention. Carter scratched his head and talked to him.

Late in the afternoon a pair of slow footsteps echoed down the hall. They were heavy, as if carrying something or someone. He heard a door open and close across the hall. Dr. Henry.

An hour later, a dinner of lamb and vegetables swimming in a spicy broth was delivered. Carter ate the hearty meal but saved some of the lamb chunks. Those he gave to

Wizard who swallowed them whole.

After night had fallen in a dense curtain of black, he heard Lyudmila's whisper outside his window.

"Carter! I've got it!"

He went to the window and reached out a hand for the backpack.

"Not yet," she said, pulling the pack out of reach. She'd found lipstick somewhere, and again a garish red slash decorated her lips. "First we do my part, then you can have the backpack."

He shrugged. He had little choice. He told her which buttons to push to fulfill the code she told him for the Bulgarian premier's office.

She explained herself first to the secretary in a soft, intimate voice full of promise. The secretary put her through to the premier, and again she talked.

"*Da*, Gelassi will give it to the Russians. Then where will you be?"

She listened, her crimson smile broadening. When she ended the call, triumph was in her eyes.

"Dawn," she said. "They'll be here then. They liked the idea!" She was full of herself, almost hopping in place with delight. She'd be a heroine yet.

"And my payment?" Carter said, already knowing the answer.

"Ha!" she chortled and threw the backpack away on the ground. "I don't need this anymore. Or you!" She slipped the tiny radio into her skirt pocket. "Stare at your supplies and dream, Killmaster!"

She flounced away around the corner of the building, her future bright with prospects.

Carter laughed quietly to himself.

"Wizard," he called.

The dog bounded to the windowsill, tail wagging. Carter threw the pillowcase ball on top of the backpack.

"Fetch!" he commanded.

Eagerly the dog lunged after the ball and brought it back. Carter scratched his head and rubbed his muzzle.

His hand empty, Carter threw an imaginary ball to the same spot on the backpack.

"Fetch!"

Wizard cocked his head, looking quizzically from Carter to the backpack and back to Carter.

Carter pushed the dog's head out the window.

"Fetch!"

The former wonder dog was uncertain, not stupid. The only man-smelling object on the ground was the backpack. He walked to it and sniffed.

"Fetch!"

Tail wagging, the dog pounced, wrestled the backpack into his powerful jaws, and proudly carried it to Carter.

Carter took the pack and petted the Doberman. The dog snuffled into Carter's hand. He liked being an ordinary dog again.

Carter walked to the bed and checked through the pack. No weapons and the radio was gone, but all else was there. He cut open a corner of the straw mattress, stuffed the pack in flat and neat, and folded over the mattress seam.

He stretched out on the bed and closed his eyes. Now he must rest. His nerves were jumpy, tense with the strain of the last few days. The mission was coming to a close. Tomorrow morning he would know whether his careful planning would bring success, or whether Gelassi would move faster and defeat him.

NINETEEN

The sky was still black when Nick Carter's internal alarm went off. He awoke in the quiet room and listened. Insects and birds sang, announcing the coming sun. In the hall outside his door, his guard stomped his feet, trying to keep himself awake at the loneliest time of the watch. Somewhere in the distance sheep bells clanged as the animals were shepherded to predawn pastures.

Carter arose and took out his supplies.

First he wrapped the striated tape around the tops and bottoms of the window bars. He scraped his nail over the tape. Instantly there was a sizzling sound and the smell of ozone. He picked the bars from the window and slid them under the bed. On the horizon, the glow from the rising sun was paling the sky into gray. Carter put the tape back into his backpack and slid his arms through the pack's straps. He slung it onto his back.

He walked quietly to the door and tapped.

"What?" came the gruff voice, hushed to not disturb the sleepers in the hallway's rooms.

"Latrine," Carter said.

It was a request the Bulgarian could understand, and he didn't want to have to clean up after any emergencies in the room. The door swung open.

Carter stepped out. The hall was empty. Snoring came from behind some of the doors where Gelassi's head men slept.

"You all right?" Carter asked the sleepy DS man with pretended concern. "Your gun loaded, ready for anything?"

The man glanced with uncertainty at the rifle. He'd been so busy keeping himself awake that he'd thought of nothing else. The momentary distraction was all Carter needed.

He slammed a rock-hard hand into the man's neck.

The rifle dropped. Carter caught it in midair.

The man slumped, then recovered, coming up with his fist. He missed, hitting Carter a sliding blow to the cheek.

Carter spun the off-balance guard around, wrapped his muscled arm around the neck, and jerked once.

The man quit breathing, brain dead. No more games.

Carter picked him up and carried him silently into the room. He laid him on the cot and covered him with a blanket, his back turned so that anyone who opened the door would see only a sleeping body.

Quietly Carter padded across the hall to the door where he'd heard Dr. Henry being carried the night before. It was locked. He pulled out his toothpick-lockpick, ran it over the tumblers, and opened the door.

The room was identical to his, a cot the only piece of furniture. The tiny figure of Dr. Henry was rolled into a ball at the edge.

Carter held her shoulder and spoke in a husky whisper.

"Dr. Henry. Nancy. It's Nick."

"Oh!" Her cry was sharp and frightened.

"You have to be very quiet," Carter went on urgently. "If you're not, I'll have to knock you out. No chances this time."

She looked at him, puzzled. He helped her up, his hands gentle. She was a brave woman. Slowly she began to think.

"You came . . . today?" she wondered.

"Yesterday." He helped her across the room. "Remember?"

"I . . . think so."

He opened her door and led her across the hall to his room. He left her there and returned to close her door. When he was back in his room, his door closed, he found her huddled and whimpering on the floor.

"Come on," he said. "You're escaping."

"I am?" she said in a tiny voice.

He picked her up and carried her to the window.

"I'll help you through first," he explained. "You wait beside the window. No need to be afraid. I'll be right behind you."

He turned her over on her stomach and slipped her legs through the opening. The sky was turning pink. Soon the fighting would begin in the sleeping valley. It was planned to be hand-to-hand combat, just enough to make the doctor's escape permanent, eliminate the guards patrolling the AWACS, and clear the runway so that Carter could fly the jet out. It was a simple series of acts that could go wrong at any point.

"I'm getting out," the doctor mumbled to herself.

"You're going to fly out," Carter said as he held her hands while she balanced her feet on the ground. "We'll fly your jet back to Geilenkirchen where it belongs."

"Good," Dr. Henry announced. "That's the right way to do it."

Carter hoisted himself up on the windowsill.

Suddenly Wizard awoke. The surprised dog saw Dr. Henry immediately. A stranger. He barked.

"Wizard!" Carter said, dropping to the ground. "Out!"

The Doberman didn't notice Carter, his gaze glued to the small trembling woman who pressed herself into the wall.

The dog snarled, then lunged at Dr. Henry.

She turned and gave a blood-curdling scream, her hand to her throat, her face pressed into the wall.

Carter grabbed Wizard's tether. The big dog barked louder. The doctor screamed more, her nerves shattered. Shouts erupted from the sleeping quarters in the building and from the tents that spread on either side of it.

"Damn," Carter said. "Wizard, out!"

It was already too late, but the dog quieted, licking Carter's hand for forgiveness. The woman slid down the wall, weeping. Feet thundered. The shouts increased. Gunfire echoed from the landing area.

"Come on!"

He picked up the doctor, threw her over his shoulder, and ran as Metodi stuck first his head, then his gun, out the now barless window. He fired. Carter dodged and ran behind a tent.

Quickly Carter took in the situation. Bulgarians were hopping outside their tents, pulling on their pants, their rifles already swung across their backs. On the landing strip, gray smoke and orange bursts of fire showed where the Macedonians had partly cleared the takeoff area. Surprised Bulgarians had engaged them in battle. On the mountainside behind Carter a dead DS guard lay spread-eagled, blood clotting his thick coat. Two dozen guards lay dead and exposed around the valley's walls. Gelassi had sent out twice as many as Carter and Petit had seen yesterday morning, enough guards to spot a sneak attack by the Macedonians. But the guerrillas were used to this kind of silent, predatory fighting. They'd eliminated the DS sentries and had been able to do quite a bit of work undisturbed on the landing strip. Now they were too busy fighting to do anything more.

Carter needed to get to the AWACS jet.

"Nick? Mr. Carter?" the doctor said from his shoulder. "Could you put me down now?"

Her trembling had stopped, but Carter needed to move fast. He adjusted her weight.

"Soon," he told her.

Carter slipped around the tent, darted between two more, and dashed behind the GAZ truck. The doctor wrapped a hand around his neck and clutched him tightly.

The sentries patrolling the jet hadn't left their posts. They watched anxiously as the fighting moved up the valley toward the headquarters building, but they kept to their rounds. Carter set the doctor on the ground next to the truck's back wheel.

"Stay here," he told her.

"I won't move," she said as he looked off. "And thank you for . . . everything!"

"No trouble," he said, dropping flat.

He shimmied under the truck toward the ankles that belonged to Metodi.

"I know he's around here s-somewhere!" Metodi said angrily. "I w-want him. F-find him f-fast!"

Three pairs of feet ran in different directions.

"I'll be w-w-waiting, d-d-dammit!" The more Metodi's rage grew, the worse his stutter became.

Carter counted to ten, rubbed his hands together, grabbed the ankles, and yanked.

Metodi fell in a cloud of dust, spluttering.

Using his tremendous strength, Carter dragged the Bulgarian killer under the truck before he could call for help.

Metodi kicked, then slammed a perfectly aimed fist into Carter's jaw.

Carter's head rang. Pain flashed red.

He smashed his free fist into Metodi's jaw.

Metodi shook his head, a tough fighter. His eyes burned with rage. The men lay on their sides, each with only one hand free.

Carter threw another slashing punch at Metodi.

Metodi deflected it with his arm and dropped his hand in an ineffectual slap at Carter's cheek. They were getting nowhere fast.

Carter grabbed Metodi's collar tight around his neck.

Metodi swung back his fist to punch again.

Balancing on his hips and elbow, Carter jerked the collar. He swung Metodi's head up and crashed it into the truck's axle.

Metodi's hand dropped to his side. His eyes widened. Scarlet blood poured down his face.

"S-shit," the DS man said.

"Some days are like that," Carter commented.

Then he bashed the Bulgarian in the jaw.

That was it. Metodi gave a little nod of concession, his pocked face surprised and disappointed. He keeled over. He'd be unconscious for hours, and with luck he wouldn't like what he awoke to.

Carter slid back to where Metodi had been, picked up the AK-47, and then returned under the truck to the doctor.

"Now we'll try for the jet," he told her.

He helped her to her feet and bent to put her on his shoulder again. The roar of four helicopters sounded in the distance.

"Well, *mon vieux*, where have you been keeping yourself?"

Carter stood, the doctor on his shoulder. The two turned to look at Henri Petit as he slipped up to them among the tents.

"Sorry," Carter said, smiling. "I've been busy."

Petit took in the heavy-soled feet of Metodi under the truck and Dr. Henry slung over Carter's shoulder. He patted Carter's other shoulder.

"So I see." The Frenchman grinned. "We have, too. But, alas, more Bulgarians are coming." He waved his hand at the helicopters. "Replacements. It is time to flee."

Carter looked down toward the landing strip and saw the Macedonians slowly retreating up the mountainside. It had been the bloodbath that Gelassi had promised. Dozens of Macedonian and Bulgarian bodies lay maimed or dead on the ground. The DS were pursuing the remaining Macedonian guerrillas up the valley walls.

"Better take the doctor with you," Carter decided. He stood her on the ground again. "She'll be safer. I still have to get to the jet, and the sentries seem disinclined to budge. Soon they'll be reinforced, too. I may never get the jet out of here."

"No!" Dr. Henry objected. "I stay with *you*!" Her eyes pleaded with Carter.

"What about Gelassi? The others?" Petit said.

"It's best if you go with Henri," Carter explained to the doctor. "You have a better chance of making it. He'll take good care of you. Ask him about his intuition."

"What about *my* intuition?" Vera said, sliding down the mountainside.

Her face was scratched from fighting. Blood stained her fingers. A Macedonian guerrilla came down with her. Quickly she introduced him as her Yugoslav lieutenant, the best man the mountains had ever known. The roar of the helicopters grew louder.

"We must leave!" she said. "Immediately! No time to get the jet!" She checked her watch. "Five minutes and my people will disappear. It's either that or be captured. Those helicopters are from Sofia. There will be too many of them to fight!"

"Take the doctor," Carter said firmly. "I don't have time to argue. Get her out of here safely!"

"No!" Dr. Henry said.

Carter shook his head and shoved her at Petit.

"Carry her if you have to. She's weak."

He picked up the AK-47 again and slipped around the GAZ truck. DS helicopters were landing near the headquarters building. Men poured out of them. Gelassi appeared in the headquarters doorway, an ironic smile on his face and a Luger held loosely at his side.

Darting from tent to vehicle to tent, Carter approached the big AWACS. The sentries' attention was now riveted on the new Bulgarian soldiers and DS men who were spreading out over the compound.

Carter skirted the bulldozer and crouched.

A man in his mid-seventies, his face severe, stalked off a helicopter and glared at Atanas Gelassi. It was Todor Zhivkov, head of the Bulgarian Communist Party since 1954 and president of Bulgaria since 1971. Next to him stood his number-two man, Grisha Filipov, premier since 1981. A big smile on her pudgy face, Lyudmila ran out of the headquarters behind Gelassi and toward the two powerful men.

The AWACS sentries were in a semicircle around the jet, staring at the action in the compound. Carter had planned well. The man who stood behind the others was directly in front of him. Carter darted out and bashed the handle of Metodi's gun into the sentry's head. Silently he dropped.

The tension had made the other sentries more alert than usual. First one turned, then the others. The five ran at Carter, the consuming excitement in the compound forgotten.

On the far side of the jet, a rifle exploded. One of the sentries fell. Vera raised her rifle and waved.

Carter didn't have time to respond.

He shot the most distant one. The Bulgarian arced over backward, blasted by the powerful AK-47. Blood spouted up out of his chest.

Gunfire rang around Carter from the other sentries. He dodged and ran around the jet, dust flying up behind him. A bullet tore through the flesh of his upper arm. The three remaining sentries raced after him, loud barking behind them.

The jet's door was open. The motors roared into action.

Swiftly Carter turned, knelt, and fired instantly, his aim true.

Two more Bulgarians flew backward, their arms outspread, shock at their mortality on their faces as blood spurted from their chests.

The last DS sentry froze, knowing his fate at Carter's hands.

A long brown streak of snarling dog fell upon the last sentry. Wizard ripped open the man's throat in the quick natural gesture of a predator. A bullet would have been faster, less painful. The man fell back, raw red flesh exposed to the morning sun. Blood spouted up, a geyser from the jugular, and sank into the dirt.

Carter ran up the stairs into the jet. Wizard chased him, barking happily. Both of them inside, Carter slammed the door and locked it.

"Help!" Vera called from the cockpit. "I can get this thing started, but after that I'm lost!"

Carter fell into the pilot's seat and moved the controls. The high-tech jet responded instantly.

"Good God," Vera said with wonderment. "A dog."

"Pet him," Carter said as they taxied forward. "He's done a good job."

Wizard sat between them, panting, his tongue hanging out and his tail sweeping the floor. His tether flopped at his feet, the end chewed through.

GS men and soldiers fired volleys at the jet as it passed. The men fired and ran alongside. Their rifles filled the air with bullets.

In the compound, Zhivkov and Filipov ignored the ineffectual battle. They were lecturing Atanas Gelassi. He shrugged, his head held high and stubborn. He'd lost, and he knew it, but he chose to go out with grace. It was the intelligent thing to do. Life wasn't worth living now.

Zhivkov shrugged and gestured at Filipov. Filipov took Gelassi's gun and pointed it at the upstart's heart.

Gelassi smiled knowingly.

Filipov did his job. He fired.

Gelassi's legs buckled. He fell into the dust of his plans, bested by those whose intellects couldn't compare to his genius.

A bullet, then two, cracked into the AWACS's windshield.

"Nikola!"

Carter pressed the controls, and the jet picked up speed down the airstrip, knocking over trees left behind by the Macedonian guerrillas. The DS men and soldiers were behind the jet now, no longer bothering to fire. They would be occupied with reinstating themselves with Zhivkov.

The AWACS lifted its heavy body up, trembling

slightly as if reluctant to leave the ground. Then it soared, a smooth and perfectly tuned beast whose natural habitat was the air.

Carter circled the jet over the valley. Below, the Macedonians were slipping off, as natural to the landscape as other native vegetation. A small group of them stopped on a distant rise, and Carter flew the jet over them. He dipped his wings. It was the French agent Petit, Dr. Henry, and four guerrillas. They waved, and Carter rocked the AWACS's wings in salute.

Vera sat back in her seat and sighed deeply. She touched Carter's sleeve.

"Where to now?" she asked.

"Ever been to Germany?" he said. "The hotels are great there."

DON'T MISS THE NEXT NEW NICK CARTER SPY THRILLER

THE VENGEANCE GAME

To Carter this smelled like a setup. But it was one he could not ignore. If the Libyans were planning on starting something here in New York when Qaddafi arrived, he wanted to know about it.

A big boat hooted out on the bay as Carter jumped up on the loading docks and stepped just within the warehouse. There were a lot of crates piled up on row after row of pallets. There was a lot of money in merchandise sitting here in the open without a guard.

Carter pulled out his Luger and flipped off the safety. He skipped across an aisle and stopped short within the shadows behind a stack of crates. He studied the labels of the boxes. There were canned hams from Denmark, some wine from France, and farther back in this row, there were more crates from Marchand Imports.

More guns.

Carter rapped on the top crate of a short pile. Then he shoved against it. The big box moved easily. It was empty. It meant the weapons had already arrived and had already been distributed.

But where? Here in New York as he was being led to believe? It was too damned pat. If Yamun was involved, and apparently he was, there was definitely something more to this business than was apparent on the surface.

Carter turned the corner and started down one of the back rows of crates toward the front of the building, when the big service doors rumbled shut, plunging the warehouse into darkness.

Carter slipped down another aisle, then circled back toward the center of the main storage area.

There was someone to his left and behind him, as well as over toward the service doors.

Carter holstered his Luger, his eyes now becoming accustomed to the darkness so that he could at least see some shadows, and climbed up on a crate. From there, very carefully and very quietly, he continued up the stack, working his way higher and higher, and closer to the service doors.

He stopped at one point and held his breath as someone hissed below. A moment later someone else answered with the same sound toward the doors.

Carter continued to the edge of the pile, then flattened himself against the crates. He took out Wilhelmina. There were two men crouched by the service doors. A third was directly below, peering around the corner, and Carter was certain he could hear two others in the back rows.

He looked back the way he had come, a tiny sound catching his attention, in time to see the vague silhouette of a man climbing up on the pile of crates.

Keeping flat, Carter scrambled carefully off the side of the pile he was on, working his way down into the stacks.

Again he holstered his Luger, and this time he slipped out his stiletto. Unless he could get them all in one spot at the same time so he could use his gas bomb as he had in Paris, he'd have to pick them off one by one.

The razor-sharp blade gleamed dully in the dim light as Carter held it at the ready.

Suddenly, he could hear the man breathing a couple of feet away, and just above. The stack of crates swayed slightly. Carter tensed. There could be no noise.

The man was directly above him now, crawling toward the edge. He had a gun in his right hand. When he had almost passed, Carter sprang up like a caged tiger, coming up behind the man, his left arm in a powerful grip around the man's head, his hand clamped over the man's mouth, and he drew the blade of the stiletto across the man's throat, blood suddenly gushing.

The man's gun clattered a few feet down on top of the next lower crate. Carter waited until the man's body stopped twitching, and then he eased it down.

Someone was below, in the aisle. "Pete?"

Carter came to the edge, but he held back. He made the hissing sound.

"Pete?" the man below whispered.

Carter dropped over the edge, directly behind the man. The surprised man spun around wildly, and Carter drove the stiletto into his heart with his right hand while grabbing the front of his jacket with his left.

The man grunted softly, shuddered once, and slumped to the concrete floor. The odds were getting better.

Carter wiped the blade on the man's jacket sleeve, then turned and hurried back into the deeper shadows of the rear aisles. Unless he was mistaken, one more person lurked back there.

They ran into each other literally, as Carter started around the corner.

The man was in his mid- to -late forties, and looked as if he had worked the docks all his life. He carried a wicked-looking loading hook in his right hand.

"Christ," he swore, backing up. He swung the hook, but Carter managed to back up just out of its range.

But the longshoreman charged again. Carter stepped

inside his range and clipped him neatly on the jaw with a left hook.

The man's head snapped back, and his legs started to buckle, but he recovered, swinging out with the hook and catching the sleeve of Carter's jacket, yanking him off-balance.

"PeeWee! Kid!" the longshoreman shouted.

Carter feinted left, away from the hook, and then back to the right as the deadly tool missed him by an inch. He drove inward and up, the stiletto deflecting off the man's breastbone and slipping between his ribs, puncturing a lung. Carter viciously yanked the blade left, then right, opening the man's chest, blood and flecks of foam whooshing out of the cavity like air from a burst balloon.

Carter was covered with blood. He turned in a half crouch as one of the other men came around the corner with what appeared to be an Uzi in his hands.

"Jesus H. Christ," the longshoreman swore, bringing up the Israeli submachine gun.

Carter dove left into the protection of the stacks as all hell broke loose, the gun nearly deafening in the confined space. Pieces of wood tore from the crates, and bullets ricocheted off the concrete floor.

He sheathed his bloody stiletto, yanked out his Luger, and quickly scrambled to the next aisle.

The warehouse was deathly still for a long time. In the distance, outside, Carter was certain he could hear sirens. Were they coming here in response to the fight? Not unless someone had tipped them off. In any event, there wasn't much time.

"Your friends are dead," Carter called out. He peered around the edge of the stack. There was no one in the aisle. He slipped across into the next row.

"I don't want to hurt you," he called out. "I've come for Yamun."

Someone was behind him. The crates above him exploded in a fury of shots. Carter rolled right as he snapped off two shots, at least one of them hitting the longshoreman with the Uzi, who fell back against the crates and collapsed, the submachine gun clattering to the floor.

"You're next," Carter shouted angrily. The sirens were coming much closer now. There were a lot of them.

"I don't want you. I want Yamun," Carter shouted.

"I don't know no Yamun," someone shouted from near the service doors.

"Who picked up the guns from here?"

"I don't know. I don't know!" the longshoreman shouted. He was frightened; it was clear from his voice.

"I don't want a fight. I just want information," Carter said, edging closer toward the front of the building.

Something fell to the floor—it sounded like a gun—and the service door slid open, the warehouse suddenly flooding with light.

"No!" Carter shouted. He jumped up, skidded around the corner into the main aisle, and raced out onto the loading docks.

There were at least a dozen police cars parked at every angle. More sirens sounded in the distance. At least two dozen policemen, all of them with their guns drawn, crouched behind their cruisers, below the loading dock, and on either side of the loading doors. The longshoreman Carter had chased outside lay flat on his face in the dirt, his arms and legs spread.

"Don't move! Don't move!" one of the officers at the door shouted.

Carter stood stock-still, his Luger in clear sight.

"You're next," Carter shouted angrily. The sirens were coming much closer now. There were a lot of them.

"I don't want you. I want Yamun," Carter shouted.

"I don't know no Yamun," someone shouted from near the service doors.

"Who picked up the guns from here?"

"I don't know. I don't know!" the longshoreman shouted. He was frightened; it was clear from his voice.

"I don't want a fight. I just want information," Carter said, edging closer toward the front of the building.

Something fell to the floor—it sounded like a gun—and the service door slid open, the warehouse suddenly flooding with light.

"No," Carter shouted. He jumped up, skidded around the corner into the main aisle and raced out onto the loading docks.

There were at least a dozen police cars parked at every angle. More sirens sounded in the distance. At least two dozen policeman, all of them with their guns drawn, crouched behind their cruisers, below the loading dock, and on either side of the loading doors. The longshoreman Carter had chased outside lay flat on his face in the dirt, his arms and legs spread.

"Don't move! Don't move!" one of the officers at the door shouted.

Carter stood stock-still, his Luger in clear sight.